"You can't keep [...]
to cost you you [...]
Wendy clasped [...] **You have to
know when to cut your losses on a bad
bet. I'm not worth it."**

"Something bad brought us together. Something
worse separated us. Now this, but it's not your fault.
And I'm never going to sit back and let someone
hurt you."

"Because of some stupid promise you made to my
brother?" Dutch had taken the vow to heart, seen
how much Jagger loved her and pleaded with
their mom to back off. She hadn't, thinking their
relationship was too intense, too all-consuming
for someone Wendy's age. So, a month after her
eighteenth birthday, two weeks before Christmas,
Wendy moved in with Jagger, and her mother's
fears became radioactive.

"No," Jagger said, "not because of your brother."

"Then why?"

He lowered his head. "I guess I can't help myself
when it comes to you."

UNSUSPECTING TARGET

JUNO RUSHDAN

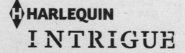

To J, my hero and the love of my life.

Recycling programs
for this product may
not exist in your area.

ISBN-13: 978-1-335-40181-6

Unsuspecting Target

Copyright © 2021 by Juno Rushdan

This edition published by arrangement with Harlequin Books S.A.

For questions and comments about the quality of this book, please contact us at CustomerService@Harlequin.com.

Harlequin Enterprises ULC
22 Adelaide St. West, 40th Floor
Toronto, Ontario M5H 4E3, Canada
www.Harlequin.com

Printed in U.S.A.

Juno Rushdan is the award-winning author of steamy, action-packed romantic thrillers that keep you on the edge of your seat. She writes about kick-ass heroes and strong heroines fighting for their lives as well as their happily-ever-afters. As a veteran air force intelligence officer, she uses her background supporting Special Forces to craft realistic stories that make you sweat and swoon. Juno currently lives in the DC area with her patient husband, two rambunctious kids and a spoiled rescue dog. To receive a FREE book from Juno, sign up for her newsletter at junorushdan.com/mailing-list. Also be sure to follow Juno on BookBub for the latest on sales at bit.ly/BookBubJuno.

Books by Juno Rushdan

Harlequin Intrigue

A Hard Core Justice Thriller

Hostile Pursuit
Witness Security Breach
High-Priority Asset
Innocent Hostage
Unsuspecting Target

Visit the Author Profile page at Harlequin.com.

CAST OF CHARACTERS

Wendy Haas—She's the owner of an up-and-coming PR firm with everything going for her until she ends up on the hit list of a cartel boss. She's surrounded by contract killers, and the only person she can trust is the one man who has every reason to hate her.

Jagger Carr—As a convicted felon working for the powerful drug cartel Los Chacales, he keeps his distance from Wendy, the love of his life. When Wendy becomes the target of the cartel, he's determined to protect her, no matter the cost.

Horatio "Dutch" Haas—Wendy's brother. Former Delta Force operator, he's part of the US Marshal's Fugitive Apprehension Response Team and is currently off the grid in hiding with Isabel Vargas.

Emilio Vargas—The head of Los Chacales. He has a vendetta against Dutch and has Wendy in his sights.

Isabel Vargas—The daughter of Emilio Vargas and Dutch's girlfriend.

The Brethren—An organized unit of contract killers for the cartel.

Maximiliano Webb—An FBI agent who once worked undercover to put Emilio Vargas behind bars.

Chapter One

Laughing at her escort's flirtatious comment, Wendy Haas glanced across the crowded reception hall of the gala and froze as she spotted trouble incarnate.

The bubble of amusement in her chest burst and she struggled to breathe. Staring back at her was *Jagger Carr*. The one man who could derail her life, for a second time.

His dirty blond hair was shorter, the cut cleaner. Half his face was cloaked in shadows, but he looked older, more rugged and chiseled by hard times. He was broader and taller than Wendy remembered, his muscled body filling out his tux to perfection.

No doubt about it, that was Jagger.

How? He was supposed to be locked up—a fifteen-year sentence for murder.

A murder that never would've happened if they hadn't been together. A prison term that was her fault.

He hated her as much as she hated him, but how could he have the gall to be in the same room as her, make eye contact and not bother to say a single word? Even one of contempt.

"Hey, babe, are you okay?" asked Tripp Langston, her on-and-off lover. "You look like you've seen a ghost."

If only. A phantom couldn't do any harm.

But Jagger free and in the flesh could wreak all kinds of havoc.

Wendy made a pleasant humming sound, masking the lead weight in her gut. "I'm fine," she said as if she didn't have a care in the world and turned back to Tripp.

The photographer dressed in a simple black suit with a dark shirt circled closer. He'd been prowling about them shortly after she and Tripp had arrived. She believed he was one from *Page Six*. Since she hadn't been up to dealing with a sensational tabloid tonight, she hadn't gotten close enough to see his badge clearly.

"He's just going to keep stalking us until we give the paparazzo what he wants," Tripp said.

It was the least of her concerns, though inevitably true. The bloodhound wasn't going to stop.

Wendy owned an up-and-coming PR firm that worked miracles in the image consulting department. She was the go-to person if you needed to reinvent yourself, as she had done after Jagger sent her world in a tailspin.

At twenty-eight, her career was on a trajectory into the stratosphere, and her name opened doors that made socialites envious.

As for Tripp, he was on the current cover of *New York Magazine*, named number one on a list of the top thirty under thirty in the city. All thanks to her company rebranding him from a barracuda in a toilet bowl to the Orca of Wall Street.

A photograph of them together would have the readers of the gossip site and tabloid talking. Still, the last thing she needed to worry about was ducking a shutterbug. Not when Jagger Carr was lurking somewhere in the room.

"Let's just get it over with." Wendy tucked her handbag under her arm and swept a hand over her hair, checking her chignon was in place.

Then she looped her arm through Tripp's, pasted on a saccharine smile, raised her champagne flute and posed for the camera.

The photographer adjusted his telephoto lens, snapped the picture and blew a kiss of thanks.

"He didn't bother to use a flash," she said, irritated at how the photo would turn out in the low lighting. *What a waste.*

"Let me get another for Instagram, babe." Tripp held his camera phone up, shifting it to get the best angle for both his six-foot frame and her standing at five feet six inches in heels. Wendy turned her face, giving her profile for the shot, and drained her glass of champagne as Tripp captured the moment with a bright flash. "That's a good one. I'll send it to you, so you can post it, too. This time write something that makes me sound fun and hip. Okay."

Handsome, wicked smart and wealthy, Tripp was a catch by many standards. He was also the walking definition of an egomaniac, always trying to tell her how to do her job. That was precisely why they were currently in off mode. They'd decided to go together to the Youth Literacy Gala—one of the most anticipated nights on New York City's cultural calendar, second only to the Met Ball—but there were no amorous strings attached.

Disentangling herself from Tripp, Wendy glanced over her shoulder.

Watching her back was second nature and came with the job. Once you identified a threat it was best to deal with the problem head-on, before it became a headline that had tongues wagging.

Wendy scanned the crowd, but it was as if Jagger had never been there. *Poof.* He'd vanished into thin air.

For a long moment, she doubted he'd been real. Only a figment of her imagination, perhaps her eyes playing tricks in the dreamy rose-tinted lighting that reflected off the marble surfaces. But the way her pulse had kicked and her nerves had danced when she'd locked eyes with him had been bona fide and irrefutable.

No other person had ever given her an inkling of butterflies, whereas being with Jagger had been like riding the ultimate roller coaster, the wind rushing over her, arms raised recklessly in the air, her heart doing somersaults, her body tingling. Not a single thought in her head of what was at stake. Of her mother's desperate pleas. Of her brother's warnings.

Until it had ended.

Her throat closed at the memory of all the tears she had shed over him ten years ago.

Wendy grabbed a glass of champagne from a passing tray, swapping it for her empty flute, and sucked the fizzy alcohol down. The chilled bubbly eased the terrible tightness in her throat, if not the sudden ache in her chest.

"What's up?" Tripp asked, typing away on his phone and staring at his screen. "You've barely had anything to drink all night, and in the past two minutes you've inhaled two glasses."

"Who are you? A ruthless cutthroat or my father?" Her dad had died when she was sixteen, a year before she met Jagger. She had still been grieving. Her brother, Dutch, had tried to step up, fill their dad's shoes, but she hadn't needed a replacement.

"You can call me daddy later if you want." Tripp chuckled at his own crass joke, and Wendy rolled her eyes as she dug her tense fingers into her satin clutch. "Let's skip dinner and cut out of this snooze fest. What do you say, babe? Your place or mine? I believe it's time to pay the piper since you signed Rothersbury."

Thanks to an introduction from Tripp, Wendy had seized an opportunity to pitch Chase Rothersbury, a bad-boy billionaire in jeopardy of losing his trust fund if he didn't clean up his image fast. After she'd given a knock-out presentation last week, she had landed her biggest client and a lucrative contract that had everyone at the gala buzzing about her.

"You're on the cover of *New York* because of me," she said, sugar dripping from her voice. "I scratch your back and you scratch mine, remember. *Babe*." How could he have possibly forgotten?

"Yeah, of course. The cover was fab." Tripp didn't even look at her as he spoke, keying away with his thumbs on Facebook or Twitter. A chirp sounded. Texting someone. "But in terms of equity, come on, there's no comparison. You owe me, right?"

All too familiar with this sport, Wendy suppressed a sigh. For Tripp, everything was a transaction, a deal he had to win. He'd tell his own mother that she owed him.

"I'm not a pink sheet stock. This feels more like arbitrage than equity." She wasn't sure if she'd gotten the terminology right and doubted herself as his eyes took on a narrowed glint.

Then she caught his shrug, a gesture of acquiescence that she attributed to his preoccupation with his phone, and she decided it didn't matter.

Off the proverbial hook, she was back on the hunt. For Jagger.

The last she'd heard he'd gotten involved with Los Chacales cartel in prison.

Which would do wonders for her reputation if old photos of her and Jagger, intimate snapshots that would make her mother screech in horror, found their way into the voracious hands of the press. At least her mom was traveling outside the country with her new husband for the next few weeks, but this was going to be resolved tonight.

What were the odds of Jagger being *there*? A million to one?

When did he get out of jail?

A better question, the one churning in her mind and making her stomach roil: What in the hell was he doing at a black-tie event for Manhattan's literati and culturati?

Unless he was there deliberately playing a sick game, taunting her with his presence. Had he come to black-mail her, extort her for hush money to keep quiet about their scandalous past?

Wendy's ears were hot, burning, as if they were on fire. As though someone was talking about her, and not in a good way. An old wives' tale, she knew, but still...

Pivoting on her heels, she turned slowly around Astor Hall. She glossed over the elaborate floral arrangements, the designer gowns, inconsequential hobnobbing and every atmospheric inch of the famed institution. Then she tuned out the jazz music and chatter in the air.

There!

Moving stealthy as a thief up the stone steps to the closed second floor was Jagger.

Jaw squared. All that muscular power striding up the stairs, looking like he'd stepped out of the pages of *GQ* instead of a cell block. God, he looked so damned good.

Hotter than a hostile ex had a right to be.

She flicked a glance at security near the entrance off Fifth Avenue. The guards were focused on an incensed late arrival who refused a pat down after setting off the metal detector.

Wendy shoved her champagne glass at Tripp. "I'll be back in a minute."

Disregarding his questions, she made her way to the broad staircase on the left.

The musical bell chimed, marking the end of the cocktail hour. The drone of voices in the room grew louder in anticipation of the early dinner. In ten minutes, the next chime would sound, and the well-dressed crowd would head for the grand hall to find their seats at the lavishly decorated banquet tables.

Perfect timing.

Appetizers should keep Tripp occupied long enough for her to have the conversation with Jagger that was a decade overdue. Tell him how much she loathed him. Then she'd send him scurrying back to whatever hole he had crawled out of, before he had a chance to do any serious damage.

No matter what it took.

She'd worked too hard putting the pieces of her heart back together, transforming herself into someone new — *better*—sacrificing everything to build her company and create a life worth living…without him.

No one, least of all Jagger, was going to bring the whole house of cards crashing down.

She darted under the velvet rope cordoning off the stairs while four guards were distracted with Mr. Upper East Side, who was now causing a scene. She lifted her rented black Cavalli gown to keep from tripping on the hem and tiptoed up the stairs, not wanting the clack of her heels to draw the unwanted gaze of the guards.

At the top of the landing, she caught the subtle sound of a door closing.

Up ahead was a sign for the lavatory. She hurried down the corridor, entered the restroom vestibule and hesitated in front of the men's door.

All the other guests were downstairs, and she'd already seen and touched everything Jagger had to offer. Clenching her jaw, she shoved inside and found an empty two-stall bathroom. No one at the urinals or sinks.

"Jagger?" she muttered under her breath.

Disappointment leaked through her, but outrage was quick to chase it away. She was as acutely attuned to his presence as she had been all those years ago.

He was up here somewhere. It was possible he'd seen her coming and was waiting for her in the ladies'.

She pulled open the door and went back into the vestibule.

Footfalls sounded in the corridor headed in her direction. She peeked out and glimpsed the photographer from *Page Six*.

The paparazzi never quit. Now he was going to harass her for a quote about the status of her relationship with Tripp.

She ducked into the ladies' room, only to find the small two-stall bathroom just as quiet and vacant as the other. Unease niggled at her, as if she was missing pieces to a puzzle.

Maybe she *was* losing her mind. The relentless hustle of working sixteen-hour days, the constant stress and never making time for a vacation was obviously taking a toll on her sanity. Instead of being downstairs relishing a once-a-year event, she was running around New York City's flagship public library, looking for a man who wasn't eligible for parole for two more years, seven months and three days.

Not that she was counting.

Trudging to the sink, she wished she'd stayed home, curled on her sofa watching a show on DVR, and hadn't come tonight. But getting tickets from the mayor for helping his daughter avoid a scandal had been an honor that she couldn't refuse.

Wendy checked her makeup and reapplied her lipstick.

The door swung open, and the photographer strode inside.

"Listen, I admire chutzpah," she said, zipping her purse. "I wouldn't be such a success without it, but this is crossing a line. Don't you think?" She swiveled, facing him, and her whole body tensed.

His dark eyes hardened as he kept walking toward her. She had the sudden unnerving sensation that the walls were closing in. Each confident step he took ate up the distance between them, dampening her bravado and ratcheting her pulse to an alarmed high.

She rocked back on her heels, uncertain what was happening.

Then she realized he hadn't asked for a quote, hadn't uttered a word. And he was blocking her path to freedom.

She glanced down at his press pass and read the name *Krish Kapoor*.

Ice water ran through her veins.

The Krish she knew was bald, stocky and in his fifties. The complete opposite of the twentysomething, wiry guy with a full head of hair stalking toward her, emanating menace.

Don't panic. Stay calm.

Her mind raced as she strategized options.

Simple and direct was best. She had to get back to a public space where a guard or guest could see her, where anyone could hear her if she needed to scream.

Swallowing hard, she straightened. Her mouth tasted sour with fear, and she did her darnedest not to let a flicker of it show on her face. "Excuse me, I'm sure my date is looking for me." She marched forward, brushing past him.

He caught her by the arm, yanking her to a vicious stop that left her teetering on her heels.

"How dare you." On reflex, she pivoted, twisting her arm up and around, breaking his hold. Her next instinct was to shove him out of her way, yell, run—all at once.

But he slapped her with so much force she went spinning and fell. Her head smacked against the edge of the countertop on the way down and she hit the floor. Hard.

Pain blasted through her skull, radiating to her limbs. The world tilted. She gasped for air.

Shocked and hurting, she dragged herself along the cold tile floor, trying get away. Even though there was nowhere to go, nowhere to hide. Fingernails scraped against grout as she hauled herself farther. Shaking, she feared she'd splinter into pieces from the pain.

"Sorry," he said. "I was told to rough you up first. Make it look like you suffered."

First. Suffered. The words swam in her mushy brain. She couldn't make sense of it.

What was going to happen once he was done making it *look* like she'd suffered?

Red droplets hit the white tile, streaking as she slithered toward the wall. She was bleeding. From her nose? Her lip? She couldn't tell.

Her attacker closed in with a few short steps. She had to do something, anything. Using all her strength, she kicked his leg. Her sharp heel connected with bone.

The guy swore bitterly. "Now, I'm really going to hurt you."

Inhaling deep, Wendy clawed up the wall, pulling herself upright as much as possible. She turned, shifting her butt onto the floor, and blinked through the agony ricocheting in her head. Her vision started to clear.

She put her back against the solid wall and faced her attacker.

The guy unscrewed the long lens on the camera and dumped a gun suppressor into his palm. He dropped the lens and slammed the body of the camera on the counter. The inside was hollow except for a gun. The pistol was so small it looked like a toy, but Wendy knew it was all too real.

She shook her head in confusion. "Why are you doing this?" she asked, wiping the moisture from her nose with the back of her hand. Blood smeared her skin.

"Orders."

"Whose orders?" She choked on a sob.

Wendy wasn't in the business of making enemies. Her success depended on smoothing things over, making trouble disappear, keeping people happy. She certainly didn't drive people to murder.

"Don Emilio Vargas."

The name sounded vaguely familiar, from the news. He was the nation's current biggest headline, the leader of Los Chacales cartel, arrested in San Diego. Why would he want her dead? How did he even know who she was?

The man screwed the sound suppressor onto the barrel of the gun.

Paralyzing terror swamped her. *No, no, no! I don't want to die.*

So much for work hard now and enjoy the rewards later. She should've taken that vacation to a warm, sunny tropical island, even if she had been alone. The same way she woke up and went to sleep. *Alone.*

She pushed back the fear and chaos raging in her mind. Forced herself to think.

"I have money. I—I can pay you a lot. Whatever you want." That was far from true, but this circumstance warranted any lie that would work.

"Once the Brethren have been ordered, money can't save you."

Wendy screamed as loud as she could, screamed until her throat burned and her lungs ached. Fearing that no one would hear her over the music and chatter downstairs, she kicked out again, this time striking his knee.

He grunted in pain, but he managed to raise his weapon and aimed.

Her heart clutched.

The door to the bathroom swung open and the guy spun, refocusing the barrel in the opposite direction.

Her attacker blocked her view, but he didn't shoot whoever walked in and let the door close. "Hey, man." The gun lowered. "What are you doing here?"

Oh, God. Her attacker knew this other man. The cavalry hadn't arrived. Tripp hadn't come looking for her. No one had heard her scream.

Wendy pressed up against the wall, wanting to disappear through it. A desperate whimper left her.

"I was sent as backup." The husky, masculine voice

was a shock to her senses, a lightning strike straight to her heart.

A voice that was deeper, coarser than she remembered, but nonetheless familiar. Even in the haze of panic and pain, she'd recognize it.

"You, too? How many of us did the Brethren send to off one chick?"

"By my count, a lot."

Wendy's stomach dropped. Tears leaked from her eyes as the terrible reality struck her, and the pain was too intense to bear.

Jagger wasn't incarcerated.

He *was* here…and he'd come to kill her.

Chapter Two

This was hell.

Not damnation with fire and brimstone.

Wendy wanted to wake up and find herself safe in her bed, in her Chelsea apartment, far from any danger.

"You barely messed her up, Zampino," Jagger said, stepping closer.

Zampino's position blocked her from getting an up-close look at Jagger, seeing his face, his eyes, but she stilled as horror and agony bled through her. Hell was knowing that he musttruly hate her to the bone to betray her this way. To seek brutal revenge.

"Yeah, I'm getting to it," Zampino said. "But she's a hellion."

"The two of us together will be faster and easier. You'll still get the credit for the kill, but I'll help."

I'll help.

Agony.

The words were a dagger twisting in her heart and cleaving it in two. Her brain flashed to past moments with Jagger. Kissing him. Being held by him. Making love to him. Soaking up his tender attention and devoted affection. Sharing everything. Getting so caught up in *him* that a life without him had been torture.

Wendy swallowed around the cold lump in her throat, not believing her ears.

"Please, p-please," she muttered in between uncontrollable sobs, the misery growing and spreading. "Don't do this."

Jagger had thousands of reasons to despise her—one for every day he'd spent locked up in a cage, denied his freedom and the possibilities she got to enjoy. But never—not in her darkest dreams, not in her worst nightmares—did she imagine him capable of physically hurting her, much less killing her.

Not Jagger.

Not the man she'd once given herself to completely, in every way.

Not the man who'd sworn on his life that she'd always be safe with him. That he'd protect her no matter what.

Not even after she was the cause of ruining his life.

It was clear that their history meant nothing to him. She meant nothing.

"Sounds good." Zampino tucked the gun in his waistband against his lower back as he turned to face her.

Wendy clenched her hands into fists and braced herself. Not for the pain that was to come. She prepared to punch, kick and fight with her last breath. With any luck, she'd get in a good scratch or two and have their DNA under her fingernails.

"We'll make it quick," Zampino said to her, as if he was about to do her a favor. He lowered in front of her and balanced on the balls of his feet. Unfortunately, he was smart enough to stay out of the kicking range of her foot. "Then we'll put you out of your misery." He smiled. It was a cruel expression, devoid of any kindness.

Wendy looked up, needing to see Jagger, and it was

like time slowed. He was still everything that had first attracted her. Rugged and beautiful, he didn't have the build of a hulking bruiser, but he had a formidable physique and a big presence that dominated any room. And those green eyes she'd loved so much had lost their warmth. They were severe and piercing, burning with resolve.

All those years she'd wasted, hating herself for losing him, craving him, trying to convince herself that she hated him, too. Maybe even more for pushing her away.

And after everything, her love for him had never died.

What a fool she'd been.

Zampino snatched her ankle and yanked her away from the wall. Wendy screamed, scratching at the floor. He dragged her closer, and when he started to rise, he lifted his foot as if getting ready to smash his heel into her face.

In a blur of movement, Jagger exploded into furious action. He drew something from his pocket and swept up behind Zampino. Jagger slipped a thin cord around Zampino's throat, tightened it across his windpipe and hauled him back.

The hand around her ankle slipped away and Wendy scrambled up onto her feet.

Eyes blazing with alarm, Zampino kicked at the air and clawed at the cord. His expression was frantic.

Wendy scampered backward and pressed against the wall, wanting to keep her distance from both men.

Zampino dragged his feet, swung his arms, grabbed for a hold onto a bathroom stall. His rubber boot heels caught on the tile flooring and he threw his skull back. Jagger defended against the move by keeping his head out of the way.

Clutching two plastic handles on either end of the

wire, Jagger jerked Zampino down at a lower angle where he was unable to gain any purchase. Face flushed, Zampino continued to struggle, thrashing in vain, his strained breathing turning into a gruesome wheeze.

Zampino pushed with his legs, scratching at his throat, his fingers slipping in the wetness of blood. His mouth opened as if to scream, to shout for help as she had done, but his airway was closed. He kicked the sink cabinetry, the edge of the stall frame.

It was futile. The hold was too tight, too absolute.

Jagger swung him to the right and to the left, thwarting Zampino's attempts to get free by shifting the man into unstable positions. Jagger's honed body was tense, every muscle flexed.

He dug in harder with the crude weapon, applying more pressure. His jaw clenched, his fists shaking from the strain. He dropped to the floor, getting better leverage while keeping Zampino on top of him. Rolling from hip to hip, Jagger avoided the elbows thrown at his sides.

Seconds slowed to a crawl. Heart pounding so hard that her chest hurt, Wendy stood frozen from the shock of watching Jagger kill a man. Again.

The first time hadn't been like this, deliberate, with merciless focus.

But, once more, he was taking a life because of her.

She wanted to close her eyes until it was done, but she couldn't look away, like there was some law in the universe that obligated her to bear witness.

Zampino's flailing arms weakened and finally fell to his sides. The last breath punched from his lips. His head flopped to the side and his panic-stricken eyes went vacant.

Jagger stayed on the floor with the cord around Zampino's neck for a drawn-out minute that felt like an eternity. Rocking to the side, he slid the dead body off him. The impulse to help him up came over her when he climbed to his knees, panting, but she was paralyzed.

Although Zampino was no longer a threat, a shiver of fear ran through her staring at him.

Jagger struggled to his feet. Then he lugged the dead body into one of the stalls and laid it on the floor by the toilet. Backing out of the stall, he stuffed the bloody weapon into his pocket.

The pulsing tension eased from her limbs, but she was rooted in place.

Jagger's voice drifted to her. He turned, his green eyes finding hers. "Are you badly hurt?" He sounded winded. "Are you okay?"

The answer was the same to both questions. "No." Her throat was coarse, like she'd swallowed sand.

His gaze roamed over her as he went to the sink and washed his hands. He dampened paper towels, shut off the water and hurried to her.

At six-two, his size was imposing for someone of her build, but this was the first time she had been intimidated by it rather than comforted. He towered over her when he reached for her face.

Wendy shrank back, a reflex after the threats and violence. Also, a small part of her wondered if she could trust him. Once you were part of Los Chacales, you were always a member, and for some inexplicable reason the top dog of the cartel wanted her dead.

Did that make Jagger part of the problem or the solution?

He hesitated. "You can't walk out like this. I need to

clean your face," he said matter-of-factly, but he didn't move toward her.

She glanced at her reflection in the mirror and drew in a sharp breath.

Blood was smeared under her nose and across her cheek. Tears had streaked her makeup.

Wendy nodded to Jagger, giving him the go-ahead. With her whole body trembling, she needed the assistance. Since he'd been arrested, she wasn't used to being protected and cared for. She'd had to learn to fend for herself.

The damp paper towel pressed to her face and the coolness of it brought immediate relief, jump-starting her brain. "We have to get security. Call the police."

"No. No police." His tone was sharp, no-nonsense, but he wiped her face with careful, gentle strokes. "No security."

"Why not?"

"Because they can't help you." He picked up her purse and stuffed the bloody paper towels inside. After tossing the handbag to her, he started wiping down the handles on the sink and the surface of the counter. "Some of the cops in the city are on Los Chacales payroll. It's safe to assume they were told to keep their ears posted for any calls involving you." Even as he cleaned up what he could of her blood from the floor, she suspected he was more concerned about leaving behind the DNA of a convicted felon. "Once I received the order about you, it took me less than ten minutes to figure out you'd be here tonight." He took her arm, his grip firm yet not hurting her, and started walking. "We can't linger."

They stepped into the vestibule after he wiped down the door.

"How did you find me?"

"Instagram. Your social calendar is splashed all over it in perfectly posed pictures with cute little captions."

Oh, God. Social media was a necessary evil for her job. She hated posting about her life, sharing her workouts, hangouts, whereabouts—a necessary part of the biz. As the number of her followers grew, so did the status of her clients.

"You even posted about the dress you were going to wear tonight."

They'd used information that she'd made public to find her. Anyone could, at almost any time, with her social media track record. She grew light-headed, weak-kneed and swayed.

He caught her by the waist and brought her up against him. His arms were hard and possessive around her, steadying her on her feet as well as something inside her. The world stopped spinning. The raging terror and confusion settled. Her racing heart slowed. Calm stole over her.

"Take a couple of deep breaths."

She did and leaned into him, grateful for the physical support, glad of his body heat and protective instincts.

He looked her over. His intense gaze was so palpable it caressed her skin. A surprising awareness flowed between them, and she went weak in the knees again. She'd never been attracted to someone like she was to him—and had been from the moment she'd set eyes on him.

"Excellent choice on the dress by the way," he said. His features lightened.

For a heartbeat, she blocked out the gruesome images from the bathroom and let herself see the man she'd once known. He was still beyond handsome with the most gorgeous green eyes. Hair that couldn't decide if it wanted to be blond or brown. No one wore rough and tumble as enticingly as he did that tux. He always had a dark sense of danger, an edge that drew her even though reason cautioned her to pull away. There'd been a hundred reasons he'd been wrong for her and still so right.

But he was different now, too. There was a new hardness to him that made him seem out of reach even though he was touching her.

"You were an unsuspecting target, and with your social media posts you made yourself easy pickings," he said, his voice softening, hints of his Southern drawl peeking through.

Any lingering doubts about him didn't evaporate, but she was cognizant of a terrible certainty. If it hadn't been for him, she'd be dead. She had no idea what she was up against or even why. For now, she needed him.

He released her from the embrace. "We need to move," he said, and she nodded in agreement.

They left the vestibule and entered the hall. He guided her toward the side stairwell that led to a different part of the library, away from Astor Hall, where the security guards were.

"I get your concern about the cops," she said low, "not knowing who to trust, but why can't we get help from security?" The odds of them being involved had to be nil.

"The more people you come in contact with, the more you'll endanger. Security is only armed with Tasers and batons. They're collateral damage waiting to happen. We need to get out of here now before we run into the others."

Earlier he'd said that there were *a lot*.

"How many?" she asked, praying for a low, single-digit number.

"So far, I've dealt with two and half of them."

How do you deal with half a person? "What does that mean?"

"I didn't finish the one that was up here. Only knocked him out," he said as they rounded the corner headed for the stairwell. "I heard you scream and—"

A man wearing a dark gray suit swept in front of them from the intersecting corridor. He held up a gun with an attached silencer.

Jagger shoved her backward behind him while he simultaneously threw a kick. His foot connected with the other man's arm, knocking the gun from his hand.

The pistol clattered to the floor out of her reach.

Both men took up a defensive fighting stance, squaring off against the other with fists poised.

"What are you doing?" the man asked.

"You wouldn't understand, Corey."

"Try me. You took a vow. If the Brethren find out that you interfered—"

Jagger launched an elbow at Corey's head, knocking him off balance. Corey staggered a few steps, then recovered, countering with a fast jab. Jagger deflected the blow. His face became a mask of intensity and determination as the two men exchanged punches and kicks, went at each other blow for blow. Their movements were powerful, brutal and shockingly quick.

Wendy had seen Jagger work out years ago, going through martial arts katas that he'd learned before they met, but never anything this fast with another person.

Corey grunted from the latest strike and tried to spin away. But Jagger pivoted into a high roundhouse kick that struck Corey's face, sending him falling to the floor in a motionless heap.

Breathing hard and sweating, Jagger stood over the man. His brows shot together in a worried expression.

"What is it?" Wendy asked, glancing around, on the lookout for any incoming danger.

"I knocked him out earlier, came up behind him. He never saw me. I should kill him. Otherwise they'll know that it was me who saved you."

"Then why don't you do it?" she asked in a harsh whisper, never believing she'd ever utter such a thing.

It was unlike her. Rewind an hour—heck, ten minutes— and she would've screamed, *No, you can't kill him*, the thought of him doing so horrifying. The cruel words had come from a dark place of desperation. She was fighting to survive and that man on the floor was a threat. When he woke up, he might very well try to kill her again.

"I can't." Jagger shook his head, staring at the helpless man. "He's my friend."

A chill shot through her. The realization that he not only knew the people coming after her but also was friends with some of them made the situation even more terrifying.

But she clasped Jagger's shoulder, relieved the young man she'd fallen in love with was still in there. Jagger Carr would never take another person's life in cold blood. In self-defense, yes, but only if he had to. He would do anything to avoid hurting a friend and wouldn't kill an unconscious person.

"Jagger." Her voice was shaky and uncertain as she pressed a palm to his cheek.

Calling his name brought him out of his tormented trance. Lowering to one knee, he pulled out zip ties from his pocket. He restrained Corey's ankles and his wrists behind his back. Jagger patted Corey down. He found his cell phone, removed the SIM card and tossed both.

Jagger found Corey's gun on the floor and stuffed it in his waistband.

His gaze snapped up to hers as he stood. "Let's go." He held out his hand to her—a lifeline, a choice she had to make.

She took his hand. His palm was warm, comforting and so big it engulfed hers. His callused fingers were rough against her skin, his grip steely.

They hurried down the stairs side by side.

It was like déjà vu, and she was that teenage girl, following him blindly. Attached to Jagger and going wherever he led. Confident he'd keep her safe.

She also remembered the dire consequences that had ripped their world apart.

"Wait," she said when they reached the ground floor near the Forty-second Street exit. "I need answers about what's happening. Why does the head of Los Chacales cartel want me dead? Where are we going? How are we supposed to survive without help from the police? What's going to happen to you when they find out that you saved me?" The shrill questions tumbled over one another in a dizzying rush.

Jagger pursed his lips, and she could tell there were things he didn't want to say. "I'll answer all your questions. Later. I promise."

Based on experience, he'd always kept his word, but fleeing the scene of a murder was a critical moment that could not be undone. There might not be any traces of his DNA in that bathroom, but there was plenty of hers. Hair. Blood. Not to mention the problem of the Brethren.

Jagger resumed moving, his stride speeding up while he tugged her along.

"This might be a mistake." She stopped, jerking him to a halt. "Take me to the police. Sure, there are a few dirty cops out there, but I'll be safe inside a police station." She had to be, surrounded by police, right? "There's one three blocks away on Broadway. Maybe I should take my chances with the authorities."

"Not on my watch." His tone brooked no argument.

But she had to try. For his sake as much as for her own. "Drop me off at the station and walk away. You can tell your friends where I am to make things right on your end. I won't breathe a word about you to the police. I'll say someone I didn't recognize killed Zampino." She didn't want to cause trouble for him. He'd done far too much already.

As tallies went, it was looking as if she'd be eternally indebted.

"The second I interceded and chose to help you, I forfeited my life." His voice was raw and unfiltered. "I didn't step aside and call the police, because it only takes *one* dirty cop to give the wrong person the right opportunity and you're as good as dead."

Wendy's heart stuttered. She pressed a hand to her chest. Jagger's words had knocked the air out of her.

This was her worst fear. Not the part about being hunted and the kill order on her. She'd already messed up Jagger's life once. The last thing she wanted was do it a second time, but apparently that was already too late.

"You took my hand." He squeezed his fingers tighter around hers. "Let me keep you safe."

He didn't say the words: *Don't let me forfeit my life for*

nothing. Yet, it was there, hanging in the air, connecting them in a hundred different ways.

"Once I'm sure you're not in any more danger," he said, "I'll get out of your life and you'll never have to see me again."

Right. He wasn't back for good, only to help her.

A new kind of agony assailed her, along with shame. To think that she'd believed he might've hurt her. He'd shown up in the bathroom to rescue her, though, considering what had transpired the last time they'd seen each other, she didn't know why.

In her heart, she wanted him to be her hero, although she'd learned the hard way she needed to be her own heroine.

She held back, studying him. Green eyes glinted with wicked street smarts.

The only person she could completely depend on was herself, but there was an inescapable caveat. Jagger understood the code of the cartel, how they operated, who they paid off, what they controlled.

He was also the only person who could give her answers that might save her life.

What choice did she have other than to trust him? "Okay. I'll do it your way."

"We need to hurry. Run while we can. Once Corey wakes up and gets loose, he'll call the others. Then it'll be that much harder to get out of the city."

Chapter Three

Adrenaline pumped in Jagger's veins like he was in a war zone.

He'd killed another man, but Zampino had been Brethren, and Jagger didn't have authorization. That in itself was a death sentence. Even worse, more would come to hunt him and Wendy down.

But all he could think about was the sound of Wendy's voice as she'd called his name, the feel of her palm gliding across his cheek.

His chest constricted with emotion.

Years ago, while sitting in a cell, he'd given up the far-fetched fantasy of *ever* touching her again. Now here she was right beside him, close enough to kiss.

His throat tightened, and he shoved the thought of it aside.

Crouched on the balls of his feet in front of the door that led to Forty-second Street, Jagger slipped the lock-picking tools out of his pocket and he attacked the pin tumbler. First, he worked the L-shaped part into the cylinder to keep pressure on the pins. Next, he slid the straight piece into place and searched for the right angle to access the locking mechanism. He had tackled this kind of lock before and estimated it would take him thirty seconds tops.

What worried him was not knowing if the library had set the alarm on the exterior doors that weren't supposed to be in use, but he couldn't fret about that.

He glanced at Wendy. Her honey-blond hair was up in a fancy twist that showed off her gorgeous face, and her light blue eyes, set against smooth, tanned skin, burned through him. In the low moonlight, her gaze shifted from aquamarine to the color of the sky at dawn.

"You should take down that updo," he said, "let your hair frame your face. So it's not so easy to recognize you."

"All right."

One tumbler clicked into place, then a second and third. Jagger worked feverishly on the next two.

The straight tool slipped from his sweaty palm and clattered to the floor.

Exhaling in frustration, he felt around for the instrument with only dim moonlight to guide him. Trying to calm his nerves, he brought himself down from totally wired to on guard.

Wendy knelt next to him as her hair tumbled loose around her shoulders in curly waves. The smell of her perfume slid over his senses, drawing him closer. The scent was soft and sensual, sophisticated like she'd become. She grabbed the thin tool and handed it to him.

Their faces were a breath apart in the low light, her proximity adding oxygen to the fire already burning inside him. Even strung tight and prepared to do whatever was necessary to keep her safe, he was tormented with a need for this woman that had never gone away. Never eased a day they'd been separated.

As a free man there were things he wanted to say to her, things he had lost the right to say, but first they had to get out of the city and survive the night.

He took the tool and got back to work.

Any second Corey would wake up. Getting free of the zip ties wouldn't take his industrious friend too long. Once that happened, Corey would contact the Brethren and holy hell was going to rain down on Jagger and Wendy. Unless they could get somewhere safe.

Got it. The last pin gave way and the tumbler fell into place.

Standing up, he braced for the possibility of an alarm sounding. If anyone else from the Brethren was waiting outside, the noise would draw dangerous attention, giving away their position.

There was no way to avoid it. They had to take the risk in order to get out of the building.

He grabbed Wendy's hand and hit the push bar. The door swung open. No alarm blared.

Releasing a breath, he peeked outside. No one loitered in the immediate vicinity. Nothing appeared amiss, although there were plenty of places for a sniper to hide in the surrounding skyscrapers.

The one thing in their favor was that if there were more hit men lying in wait, they were most likely covering the main entrance.

They stepped into the cool night, hurrying down the steps.

"Where are we headed?" Wendy asked.

"Parking lot." Jagger led her down the block in the direction of Sixth Avenue, wanting to bolt with her like two bats out of hell, but instead he forced himself to walk. She'd never be able to run in those sexy heels, and it would only cause people to notice them when they needed to blend in. "I've got a car there."

He caught the surprised glance from her. Keeping a car in the city wasn't practical or economical.

Deciding to spare her the trouble of asking, he said, "I sort of borrowed it. I co-own a car repair shop. We do a lot of custom work." He left out the fact that the other owner was his former cell mate and that the majority of their business came from the cartel.

The service of providing souped-up vehicles that were outfitted with turbocharged engines, bulletproof windows, reinforced doors and fortified chassis to handle the extra weight proved to be quite lucrative. Though there was a small pool of clientele looking for that sort of thing and hardly any of them had legitimate reasons for wanting it.

They stopped at the corner and waited for the light to change.

Shivering, she rubbed her arms. "When did you get out of prison?"

"Are you cold?" It was April, and the fickle spring air had dropped ten degrees over the past two hours. The night wasn't frigid, but decidedly chilly.

"I'll be okay."

He pulled his shirt from his pants, covering the gun with attached silencer that was tucked against his back in his waistband. Despite her protests, he took off his jacket and draped it around her shoulders. His adrenaline would keep him warm.

"Thank you," she said reluctantly, and slid her arms into the sleeves. "How did you manage to get released early?" Her tone was sharp, almost harsh. "You're not supposed to be eligible for parole yet."

"Sorry to disappoint you." He fired back.

"Jagger." It was a plea as well as a warning. "When did you get out?"

He gritted his teeth as he checked their surroundings. Many of her questions he couldn't answer because he simply didn't know. Only the top lieutenants in the cartel had any clue why Don Emilio wanted her dead. The Brethren didn't care. They'd been tasked by the leader of Los Chacales himself. The order was sacrosanct.

Jagger was the only one who'd dare violate it.

As far as how to get out of this mess, he was winging it. The order had been short notice, not leaving time for him to fully strategize, much less contemplate the consequences that would come down the pike. His business, the life he'd rebuilt after prison were at stake, but he'd given little thought to any of it when he'd seen Wendy's name attached to the termination command. He was taking things one step at a time, weighing the pros and cons of every choice. Not to be a hero. His sole concern was keeping Wendy alive, and the one thing he knew for certain was that going to the police would be a mistake they wouldn't live to regret.

"How long ago were you released?" she asked again, her voice growing more strained.

This was one question he was capable of answering, even though it was the last he wanted to discuss. "Three years."

Gravity pulled his gaze from the steady stream of vehicles and heavy foot-traffic around them back to hers.

Without fully registering her shocked expression in the bright lighting from the streetlamp, he took in how beautiful she'd gotten. Wendy had always been a looker. Heart-shaped face. Creamy skin. Cat-shaped eyes. Flawless figure that was somehow both slender and voluptuous. But everything about her had matured and been refined. She'd gone from gorgeous to exquisite.

Still took his breath away, but now the sight of her also made his heart ache.

A second or two ticked by as the little color that was in her face drained. She stared at him, her eyes huge and features pinched with pain that was unrelated to Zampino hitting her.

"Three years," she said in stark disbelief that twisted his gut in a knot.

The impulse to hold her was overwhelming. He wanted to comfort her, kiss her, taste her lips one more time, but if he did, he wasn't sure he'd be able to walk away.

The traffic light changed, saving him from himself.

"Come on." He reached for her hand, but she folded her arms across her chest, stepped off the curb and strode into the crosswalk.

Ignoring the sting of her rebuff, he was at her side in an instant.

They rushed across the street and hurried in the direction of the parking lot in silence. Their arms brushed once or twice, and each time she put a couple of inches between them as they navigated through the evening flow of pedestrians.

"Wendy." He caught her arm, but she jerked free of his hand.

Not that he blamed her for not wanting him to touch her. Their history was messy and complicated. Too ugly to dive into if he knew what was good for him.

"Why didn't you tell me that you were out? Didn't you think I'd want to know?" Her words were barely a whisper, yet the hurt attached hit him with startling gravity.

She cared. After so many years, he still mattered to her. She hadn't buried the memory of him.

Despite the fact he'd hoped she would've forgotten him—awful as it was—a selfish part of him was relieved she hadn't.

He took extreme care selecting his next words. What sprang to mind didn't seem to fit the awkward moment or the grave situation.

Nothing was right. Everything was wrong. What was he supposed to say?

That he was sorry for not contacting her after he was released?

Well, he wasn't. Any more than he regretted the harsh things he'd said to her on her last visit to see him inside Sing Sing prison.

"You didn't have a *need* to know. It was my personal business." Staying dispassionate and pragmatic was the only viable option if he was going to figure out a way for them to get through this and survive. "I didn't think it'd make a difference to you. We're nothing to each other anymore."

"Nothing?" She choked on the word and then straightened. "The last time we saw each other, you told me that you hated me. So if we're *nothing* and that hate is still festering inside of you, why are you here?" There was no missing the anger tightening her voice.

As if he'd ever let someone kill her—regardless of their history. Hell, because of it.

It would've been a blessing if he could safeguard her without speaking at all. But that wasn't possible. Wendy would push and prod and question until he answered.

"I made your brother a vow." To always protect her. That was what Jagger had sworn to get her brother and mom to back off and give their relationship a chance. "I'm a man of my word. I'll uphold it and do the right thing whatever the risk."

He never bothered with a cost-benefit analysis when it came to Wendy. Risk versus the odds of success be damned. His intervention was a necessity. He had to find a way to keep her alive.

"You're really not here for me," she said low, as if speaking to herself.

He *was* there for her, but he preferred to downplay that part. It was bad enough he was feeling emotions he shouldn't. "This is a mercy mission." How simple, how clear-cut things would've been if that was the whole truth. If he was no longer a devil-may-care fool in love with Wendy Haas, but his actions were proof to the contrary.

Only a fool would go up against the deadliest, most powerful drug cartel on the continent, and he sure as hell wasn't doing it because she didn't mean anything.

Mercy mission. More and more it was starting to feel like a suicide mission.

"We should pick up the pace a bit if you're able." His voice was cool steel. Giving way to sentiment did no one any good.

Wendy lifted the hem of her dress and quickened her step. Her heels stabbed the pavement with a strident clickety-clack. "Why does the head of Los Chacales want me dead? And please don't give me the brush-off."

"The order came down short notice. Immediate execution." Figuratively and literally. "There weren't many details, but I think it might have to do with Dutch."

Wendy's gaze snapped to Jagger and a befuddled look fell across her face. "My brother? That doesn't make any sense. He works in fugitive recovery. I saw on the news that Vargas was only just arrested. Dutch goes after fugitives on the run, so how on earth could he have angered the head of the cartel so much that he wants *me* dead?"

Jagger shrugged, wishing he had the answers. Without insight into the particulars, he'd only be able to buy Wendy time, not save her. "The order was issued as a blood debt."

"What does that mean?"

"That this is really bad. Somebody who is very close to you must have killed or harmed an important person Don Emilio cares about. I don't know specifics. I'm not privy to that sort of information."

"These days I'm only close to my mom and…Dutch."

"I figured your brother is more likely to be connected to this than your mother. What I know for certain is that this is a life-for-a-life kind of thing. The Brethren are invested beyond money. It's a matter of honor." Under normal circumstances, Jagger could pick and choose his assignments, but no one—absolutely no one in the Brethren—could refuse a blood debt kill order.

"Honor in the cartel?" Wendy scoffed. "Give me a break. Los Chacales, those Jackals, have no regard for human decency. They're all vicious drug dealers, thieves and murderers."

His heart froze, and he blocked out the surge of pain in his chest.

Jagger hadn't spoken to Wendy in almost a decade, and the first time she saw him again, he'd wrapped a homemade garrote around someone's neck and strangled the man. He was appalled at his actions, regardless that they'd been necessary.

Another reminder of what had driven them apart

years earlier. "Yep, drug dealers, thieves and murderers. That's us."

"Oh, Jagger," she said, flicking a cautious glance at him. A glimmer of regret caught in her gaze. "I didn't mean you. I wasn't talking about you. Just them."

But he *was* them. In every way that counted. Not that it was the entire story.

"Don't worry about it," he said. "I am Los Chacales." A long, dark road paved with self-preservation had led him there. "I'm Brethren, too." They were a well-trained, highly organized lethal extension of the cartel. Not gang-bangers and foot soldiers. They were *sicarios*—hit men with specialized skills, loyal to the cartel. "We are a pack of murderers. You're right, except for one thing. There is a code in the cartel, and those who don't respect it suffer the consequences." As he would soon find out, but he'd cross that bridge when he got to it. Or burn it down. He was undecided.

A visible shiver ran through her. "Well, then, how do we fix this?"

He didn't have a clue.

Fix wasn't a part of his current plan. Only keeping them both above ground and breathing. "I'm working on it."

"Your tone doesn't inspire confidence."

"Who stopped Zampino and Corey and has gotten you this far?"

"You're right. I'm sorry. I'm scared."

One block to go and they'd have wheels. On foot out in the open on the streets left them too hideously vulnerable. Exposed. He felt like they had bull's-eyes on their backs. There was no telling how many from the Brethren were looking for them or what resources they might use. "You should ditch your phone."

"Get rid of my phone?" She stared at him like he was crazy. "Are you serious?"

"Let me rephrase. The sooner you dump your phone the better."

"It has all my contacts. My calendar. My appointments. My whole life is on my phone."

How convenient to be able to reduce the essence of your life down to what was accessible on your smartphone. "Sounds valuable," he said, keeping his voice curt, not a hint in his frosty tone of the man who'd once had all his hopes and dreams and desires tangled up in this woman.

"It is extremely valuable. I don't know what I'd do without it."

Perhaps take a break from posting on Instagram and live to see another day.

"I should point out," he said, "that if the Brethren track you through your phone, you won't have much of a life left. Correction, *we* won't. And forget about keeping any of your appointments."

Looking up at him, she let her dress slip from her hand and tripped on the hem. Instinct had him reach out and grab hold of her to keep her from falling—a hand at her waist and the other cupping her palm.

The one little gesture sent sparks of heat and electricity tingling through him, and he could have sworn he'd seen the same in her eyes, in the way her jaw unhinged and in the breath that left her perfect lips.

Once she was steady, she yanked her arm free of his grasp and tore her gaze from him in response. "No one has had physical access to my phone to download malware, and without a court order not even the FBI can get information from my mobile provider."

That was the naive thinking of a law-abiding citizen with no idea of what the underworld was capable of.

Jagger gave a bitter laugh. "We're talking about Los Chacales. The most formidable cartel in North America. How do you think they got so powerful? It wasn't by using court orders to get what they want. They circumvent the law. They have people everywhere. You name a mobile phone provider and I guarantee that they have an inside person who is looking for you in their system as we speak. When your name pops up, they'll ping your phone and will have your location within a one-hundred-fifty-meter radius. Brethren will be dispatched, and that radius will shrink until we're surrounded and dead."

She lowered her head and crossed her arms, tucking her purse along with the phone stashed inside of it in a protective position. "What about *your* phone?"

"I left it back at my place." Fingers curling in his palms, Jagger checked their rear. Still no signs of any shadowy members of the Brethren tailing them, but they needed to get to the car quickly. He had the feeling their luck was going to run out sooner rather than later. "So, are you going to scrap yours?" Or was he going to be forced to do it for her? This was his world and she was in way over her head. She needed to trust him. To follow directions. If he said run, then she had better run. If he said ditch your phone… "Decide now before we get in the car."

He stopped at the corner and gestured to the hourly paid parking lot across the street.

Huffing a defeated sigh, Wendy unzipped her glitzy purse and handed him her cell phone.

Jagger removed the battery, tossed the SIM card on the ground and raised his foot, getting ready to crush it under his boot heel.

Wendy winced. "Wait. Are you sure that's absolutely necessary?"

It wasn't. Removing the battery was sufficient to prevent the phone from being tracked, but the extra precautionary measures were the only way to be certain no one made a desperate phone call while on the run. "Do you swear to leave the battery out and not use it under any circumstances?"

Her baby blues brightened. "Yes, yes. I promise."

"Okay." He scooped up the SIM card and handed everything back to her.

Exhaling as though he'd saved her life again, she dumped the components in her purse with a shaky hand.

At the corner, they waited for a break in the traffic to get across.

A vague sense of alarm had him swiveling around, doing a 360-degree check of their surroundings. At the intersection, one block over to the east on Fifth Avenue, he spied a large black truck stopping at the traffic light. A prickle of warning slid down his spine at the familiar outline of the vehicle.

Jagger grabbed Wendy by the shoulders and whisked her back from the curb and behind a building.

"What is it?" she asked.

"I'm not sure." He peeked around the edge of the brick building and trained his sights on the truck. From that distance, he couldn't see the driver.

The traffic light changed, and the truck rolled through the intersection down the parallel avenue, heading in the direction they'd come from.

The hairs on the back of his neck raised at seeing the shiny black vehicle, an M2 Freightliner. Twenty-two-foot-long custom tactical body with metal reinforcement and a pull-down rear ramp. Interior features comprised an armory cage with enough storage for a small arsenal and custom flip-up bench seating that, when in the upright position, provided space for two motorcycles to fit on board.

Jagger knew this because he was the one who had done the custom work on the vehicle, including the installation of the bulletproof windows, and tires filled with silicone so they wouldn't go flat or get shot out.

That beast on wheels was the property of Los Chacales cartel. More specifically, it belonged to the Brethren.

Chapter Four

The tendons in Jagger's neck tightened as he cursed their rotten luck. A handful of hit men pursuing them individually was one thing. A united mobile unit following one person's direct instructions was a game changer and not in their favor.

He raked a hand through his hair. "Corey must be awake. The Brethren dispatched a mobile unit."

"How do you know it was Corey?" Wendy asked. "You trashed his phone, the same way you were about to with mine."

"But not Zampino's." In the bathroom, Jagger had been focused on a hundred different things—chiefly the blood on Wendy's face, the stark terror in her glassy eyes—and had forgotten one that was critical. Corey must have found the phone after he had gotten loose and then called in reinforcements.

Jagger double-checked that the street was clear of any immediate threats and gestured for her to follow him.

They hustled across the road, darting through a break in traffic, to the parking lot.

Digging in his wallet, Jagger fished out two twenties and paid the attendant.

They climbed into the navy Mustang, and he turned

the key in the ignition. The engine roared to life. This car was his personal pet project, loaded with all the bells and whistles and a few extras he'd never added to any previous vehicles. Another customer, a high-ranking lieutenant in Los Chacales, had spotted him finishing up the muscle car and offered to buy it. The guy had been so adamant, offering to pay more than the vehicle was worth with the upgrades, that Jagger had agreed to sell it. The new owner was supposed to pick her up tomorrow, but a customer's disappointment was not on his list of priorities.

Throwing the car in Drive, Jagger did another quick search of their surroundings before pulling out of the lot.

"Where are we going to go?" Wendy asked.

"Out of the city. Somewhere safe. Then we'll regroup and come up with a plan."

Taking the FDR Drive north was one option to reach the Upstate New York destination he had in mind, but the 495 might be faster at this time of night. Not only to get to where they were ultimately going, but also it was the quickest route out of the city.

To say that Wendy wasn't going to like it was an understatement. The 495 meant taking the Lincoln Tunnel—a tube that was a mile and a half long, less than twenty-two feet wide, ninety-seven feet below the Hudson River. For someone claustrophobic like Wendy, the short drive through would probably feel like several hours, but every minute they were in Manhattan counted and he wasn't going to waste any.

"Put your purse in the bag in the back."

Wendy reached between the seats, grabbed the black duffel and hefted it onto her lap. "This weighs a ton. What's inside?"

"Supplies."

She unzipped the duffel and peered down at the contents. "What in the hell? You had all this stuff on hand?" she asked in disbelief as if he wasn't a hit man for the cartel. Rifling through the weapons, she gasped. She held up a canister that had a pin. "Please tell me this isn't a grenade?"

"Okay, then I won't."

She shrank back in horror.

"Relax. It's only smoke, nonexplosive." Though it had a variety of uses and one never knew when it might come in handy.

Lifting what looked like, to an untrained eye, a piece of molding clay the size of a deck of cards, she said, "Are you going to tell me this causes smoke, too?"

Truth be told, C-4 did create a lot of smoke, after the explosion. "I told you to put your purse inside, not to take inventory or to ask questions if you don't really want to hear the answers."

He took a left onto Seventh Avenue, heading south. To reach the 495 they had to backtrack, and this route would take them within two blocks of the library. Dangerously close. As much as he hated that, there was no choice with the city's network of one-way streets. Since traffic wasn't gridlock, they should be able to move smoothly, and the car's windows were tinted, offering a small degree of concealment.

"What do you plan to do with all this? And yes, I want the answer."

"I don't have a plan. I just wanted to be prepared."

"Still a Boy Scout, I see. Only you're playing for the bad guys these days." Wendy stowed the plastic explosives and her purse inside the bag. After zipping it closed, she heaved it into the back.

"It's complicated."

"Which means you don't want to talk about it."

No, he didn't. Jagger tightened his grip on the steering wheel. He had no desire to dredge up the hard, ugly choices he'd had to make that led to his current predicament. Maybe a part of him was afraid she wouldn't understand. When they had been together, she'd never judged him or made him feel he had to prove himself. Things had changed. She had every right to question the decisions that had put him on the cartel's payroll as an assassin.

"I noticed a flip phone in your bag." Wendy leaned back in her seat, and her shoulders relaxed. "I thought you didn't bring one."

"It's a burner phone. For emergencies only. No one has the number. I'm not tied to a plan that can be traced, and that model doesn't have a GPS chip, so it can't be tracked."

Wendy ran her hand along the dashboard and the seats. For a long, silent moment she looked over the interior. "You restored this beauty, didn't you?"

She had always had an affinity for the things he loved—cars, the outdoors, hunting, football. Things she'd learned to appreciate from her father before he died, and her brother. But during their time together, anything that was important to him became important to her and she showed genuine interest. It was one of the things he loved about her.

"Guilty," he said, biting back a small smile. His heart warmed at knowing that she hadn't lost her eye for spotting his work. Just as quickly, he realized it might be wishful thinking on his part. She could've easily made an assumption based on the fact that he'd picked this car to drive.

"You leave a little piece of yourself in your work. Always did. I can see it in the details."

This time he let the smile ghost across his lips. That she still knew him so well gave him hope. Of what exactly, he wasn't quite sure, but even as vague as it was, he'd grab hold of it with both hands.

A right turn took them onto Thirty-seventh Street through the Garment District. Traffic slowed, growing heavier. They'd put some distance between them and the library, where he hoped the mobile Brethren unit was parked and not out searching the area.

In a few more blocks, they'd start to merge onto the 495.

"You said you own or, rather, co-own a car repair shop."

"Yeah."

His partner and good buddy, Sixty, who had earned the nickname because he could boost almost any car in sixty seconds, had an arrangement with the cartel for tricking out their rides before he had been incarcerated for grand theft auto. Jagger was a mechanic, loved tinkering with anything on wheels. At night in their cell, he came up with ways to take the upgrades to the next level. Sixty thought they'd work well together, and as it turned out they did. A match made in heaven. Or hell, considering they worked for the cartel. Jagger had increased the shop's profits three hundred percent in the first six months.

Sixty was the closest thing Jagger had to a best friend after getting released.

"Here in the city?" she asked. "In Manhattan?"

He dipped his head in response, his gut churning in

anticipation of the next question, the much heavier one that he didn't want to answer.

"Where exactly?" she asked.

He took a deep breath. Best to spit it out and let the cards fall where they might. "Hell's Kitchen."

Her jaw set hard and her eyes lifted to his.

"Your shop is in *Hell's Kitchen*." A pregnant pause swelled in the car, sucking up the oxygen. "I would've guessed Brooklyn or the Bronx. Hell's Kitchen is about what, twenty minutes from the heart of Chelsea? That's where I live, by the way."

An eight-minute car drive to get to her place from his, depending on traffic. With a bus ride on the M11, fourteen. If he took the C train and transferred to the E, it would be closer to sixteen. He was aware of which posh building, the floor and unit she lived in, and had before he'd even stepped foot out of Sing Sing.

Not seeing her didn't stop him from keeping tabs on her, ensuring that she was all right.

"Twenty-five minutes, give or take," he said, and it was true, if he was walking.

He lived above the car shop and sometimes, when he had trouble sleeping, he'd stroll the streets. Always found himself out front of her building, with gut-wrenching memories battering him while he contemplated ringing her bell.

Deep down, he realized that would do more harm than good. Regardless of how he had ended up behind bars, he was the one who had pushed her away. She didn't deserve him mucking up her situation. It was impossible for him to turn back the clock and be the man she used to know and love. That guy was gone, but if she was ever in danger, then he'd be there for her. Protect her the way he swore on his own life to Dutch that he would.

A kill order definitely constituted danger with a capital *D*.

"Twenty-five minutes, huh. From Chelsea, or my apartment specifically?" When he didn't respond, she asked, "Did you already know where I lived?"

"I'm pretty sure every member of the Brethren who received the kill order on you knows where you live. It's a good thing you weren't at your apartment earlier when I swung by there first."

"I got ready at my fashion stylist's loft." She shifted in her seat, facing him. "But that's not what I meant. Did you know where I lived before tonight?"

He didn't want to lie, but would admitting the truth make him seem like a stalker?

Good God, was he a stalker? Not the creepy kind, but one nonetheless?

His intention was to watch over her from a distance, keep her safe without intruding in her life.

"How long have you known where I live?" She put her hand on his thigh and shook him, demanding an answer.

Heat sparked from her touch, radiating up his leg. Parts of his body loosened while the rest stiffened, kicking into gear. He'd craved the feel of her touch, imagined her caress against his skin, and this simple brush of her hand left him aching for so much more.

Jagger glanced at her. Gleaming blue eyes drilled into him, penetrating past the barrier he'd erected after he'd slammed the book closed on their relationship ten years ago.

The connection between them flared, tugging at him, alive and animate. It stole his breath, but the one awful thing that had gone wrong for them was there, too. The one thing that had separated them for nearly a decade was front and center, and the pain he'd caused her was just as palpable.

"I do have a confession," he said. "And you're not going to like it." He pursed his lips, trying to ignore her enticing fingers sliding across his thigh.

"Try me."

Tempted as he was to give in to the distraction of the physical contact and get lost in her eyes, this wasn't the time or place. It was too easy to be lured into a false sense of security in the confines of the car, and in the next three seconds she was going to be furious with him. There was no telling how she'd react.

"We have to go through the Lincoln Tunnel," he blurted out. No way to sugarcoat it and there was little point trying.

Wendy reeled back, her eyes flaring wide with hollow misery. Her hand on his leg retreated and she clutched her chest. "No! Go a different way."

"Too late." He hiked his chin forward, redirecting her attention. "We're already here."

The Lincoln Tunnel lay in front of them. Long gone was any opportunity to turn around. They'd passed the last exit and were now on the ramp to the westbound portal. He merged into one of the lines funneling toward the tube about two hundred feet up ahead.

Twenty-foot-high concrete walls bracketed either side of the two lanes of vehicles. Metal lane dividers kept cars from veering off course, channeling the traffic in one direction—forward. Headed straight for the dark gaping mouth of the tunnel.

"I can't do it," she said, her voice rising. "Not the tunnel."

"You can. I'll be right beside you the entire time."

"No! I'm not going inside that death trap. I'd rather surrender to Los Chacales and let them put me out of my misery quickly."

"It'll be fine. Close your eyes and breathe through it."

"Did you read the article in the *New Yorker* that said the tunnels are the biggest targets for terrorists? The soil above the tunnel has shifted and there are cracks. What if something happens inside and—"

"Not today. The tunnel will hold." He grasped her hand and interlaced their fingers. "Take a deep breath," he said, and she did. "Another, slower."

He understood how serious her claustrophobia was. She had difficulty in elevators, which was hell in Manhattan, and avoided the subway, a more expensive kind of hell in the city. Flying was okay for her, and he suspected it had something to do with being able to see outside through the window. The tunnel, however, was intolerable.

Wendy flicked a terrified glance at the current source of her fear. He put their clasped hands on his chest, and her gaze returned to his.

"I don't know." She shook her head and squeezed her eyes closed. "I don't think I can make it."

He tightened his grip on her soft hand, needing to find a way to stem her anxiety. "Hey." The single word drew her focus back to him. "We'll make it through, together. I promise. Besides, there's no way the cartel is lucky enough for some freak accident to take us out."

She gave a small, sad chuckle. "That's a good point,"

she said. "What would be the chances? It would take insane odds. Right?"

"Exactly."

Wendy gulped and nodded slowly. "I'll try."

"Try? You're Wendy Haas. The most determined person I know when you set your mind to something. Strong and beautiful and smart. A fighter with guts, who never gives in." And it was for all those reasons that he'd been cruel to her on her last visit with him in prison.

She heaved a deep breath. "Well, that's a lot to live up to."

"Not for a tough cookie like you."

Something changed in the air as she turned her mesmerizing blue gaze on him. A hundred memories floated into his mind. Kissing her in the rain. Long chats snuggled together in front of the fire. Making love to her, consumed with a breathless need, only for her. Never wanting to let her go.

"Don't look at me like that," she said.

"Why not?"

"Because—"

The lights on the monitor below the dashboard and the instrument panel flickered. The radio turned on and pop music filled the car—Imagine Dragons' latest song from whatever movie was dominating the box office. They exchanged a surprised glance.

He released her hand and hit the button to switch off the radio.

Nothing happened. Music continued to blare, lyrics wrapping around them.

It was the strangest thing.

He stabbed the button for the radio again—the music kept playing.

"What's happening?" Wendy asked, pressing back against her seat.

"I don't know."

The radio bounced from FM to AM. Static boomed across the airwaves.

Wendy turned the dial for the volume with no effect. "What the hell?" she asked over the noise.

Suddenly the radio cut out.

Silence descended and a chill shot up his spine, but he kept a bead on their progress toward the tunnel. They were almost there. One hundred yards from the entrance.

Racking his brain for an explanation as to why his car was possessed, a terrible suspicion slithered into his head. There were two possibilities. Best case, a short in the electrical system somewhere, somehow. Worst case, they were being hacked.

These days a car was a big computer on wheels.

The Brethren employed individuals from a variety of backgrounds and skill sets, but none of them would be able to infiltrate his vehicle's system. They'd need the VIN number, engine model, to know what electrical system he was using.

Jagger looked up at the sluggish traffic.

They had to make it to the tunnel. Once they were inside, he'd know one way or the other. The structure of the tunnel provided natural shielding. If they were being hacked, the disruptions would stop until they exited on the other side, and if they weren't, the issues would persist.

Either way, he could ditch the car in New Jersey, but they had to cross through first.

Eighty yards to go. The line of cars crept forward.

Inside the tunnel, the speed limit was thirty-five miles

per hour. Their approach to the entrance with the bumper-to-bumper traffic was closer to a painful ten miles per hour crawl.

The monitor on the dashboard flipped through screens and flashed from Radio to Settings to Bluetooth. The wireless connection activated.

Sixty yards.

Trimble, the telematics system, popped up. It was a more robust version of OnStar or Teletrac Navman, which could transmit information from the vehicle to the outside world and allow an occupant to call for help.

Fifty yards.

"Jagger." The shaky male voice over the speakers gave the identity away.

Recognition sliced through him. "Sixty, is that you?"

"I'm sorry, man," Sixty sniveled, his voice tight with pain. "They're making me do it."

Jagger's heart punched into his throat. "Do what? Who's in charge?"

Static crackled through the 4G network connection. Voice mode deactivated.

"Sixty?" His stomach turned inside out. If the Brethren had control of the vehicle's telematics, they were hosed. "Sixty?" Jagger hit the Call for Help button on the screen. When nothing happened, he jabbed an impatient finger at the disconnect icon, trying to sever the connection.

The steering wheel lurched, and the brakes engaged, slamming the car to a jerky stop twenty yards from the entrance of the Lincoln Tunnel. They were close, so close.

Jagger pressed the accelerator, but nada. The engine didn't even rev in response, and the steering wheel had locked.

His heart galloping, he stomped on the gas pedal, smashing down on the accelerator in the hopes of getting the slightest movement. The car didn't budge. The gears were stuck in Park.

"Nothing is working," he said, jamming his foot on the gas as hard as he could.

Horns blared from the cars stuck in line behind them as the rest of the vehicles in front proceeded into the tunnel. Onlookers from the adjacent stream of traffic in the next lane gawked as they passed by.

"What do we do?" Wendy asked.

The monitor on the dashboard blipped from Trimble to Navigation with mind-blowing speed. A map came up on the screen.

Trimble combined a GPS system with onboard diagnostics that could cross-reference the data from the sensors in the vehicle. Within seconds, the Brethren would know the exact location of the car.

Jagger had installed the system in case of an emergency or to track the vehicle if it was ever stolen. Now his resourcefulness was being used against him, to trap him and Wendy, and someone was torturing Sixty to do it.

No good deed goes unpunished. I should've killed Corey. If he had, they wouldn't be in this bind. He shoved the thought to the back of his head.

Their coordinates were highlighted on the monitor. Latitude and longitude, degrees, minutes, down to the seconds.

Slapping the steering wheel, Jagger let loose a string of foul words. "We've got to move. We need to get out of the car."

They both tried the handles, but the doors wouldn't

open. He pressed his thumb frantically on the tiny button on the key fob even as he knew it wouldn't work.

Pushing the keyless ignition button to shut down the engine was equally as futile.

Jagger would've fired a couple of bullets at the windows, but the glass was bulletproof.

He'd been shut out of his own vehicle's system. The brakes and locks were under Sixty's control, or rather the Brethren's.

No doubt the mobile unit he'd spotted earlier was already on the move, coming straight for them. They were sitting ducks in a tin can with no way to escape.

Thanks to the bulletproof windows, the Brethren wouldn't be able to take them out with gunfire from a distance, but the alternative wasn't better. To kill them inside the car, the Brethren would have to blow it up.

Wendy scrabbled at the door handle again with no success. Jagger threw his shoulder against his door as he tried the handle, gripping it so hard his fingers hurt, and failed to get it open.

Dread constricted his chest.

Think. There had to be a solution. He couldn't let fear cloud his reasoning.

"The lock won't give!" Wendy said. "They're coming, aren't they."

Their eyes met. The terror in her gaze tore at him, but it was knowing that the longer they stayed the likelihood of the Brethren killing her increased that spurred him into action.

He released his seat belt and climbed into the back, ignoring the steady stream of agitated beeping coming from the cars jammed up behind them.

"What are you doing?" she asked.

"The trunk. That might be our only way out." Unlike the convertible Mustang model, his fastback came with flip-down rear seats. He found the first tab on the right upper corner and pulled the rear seat into a horizontal position. Once he got his hand on the second tab, he got the other seat down out of the way. "Come on."

She scrambled into the back beside him.

Jagger scooted into the trunk, feet first, hauling the bag of supplies along with him "The emergency release isn't connected to the electrical system, so it can't be controlled or disabled by anyone on the outside. I'm going to need you pull on it while I give the trunk door a good kick, since the lock is electronic." He pointed out the glow-in-the-dark T-handle latch.

To reach it, she'd have to enter the trunk headfirst. Wendy crawled in next to him, slid into position and grasped the handle.

"On my count," Jagger said, and she gave a quick nod. "One. Two. Three."

Wendy yanked the latch and Jagger kicked with both feet, giving it everything he had.

The trunk door popped up. Fresh air whooshed in over them.

He hopped outside and then helped Wendy. Slinging the bag of gear onto his shoulder, he glanced at the long line of cars clogged to a standstill.

Over the horns blaring, he picked up another sound. Motorcycle engines. Fast. High-powered.

Two sleek black motorcycles roared around the corner. The drivers wore tinted black full-face helmets, gloves and matching sinister outfits, and their bikes turned them into an even more terrifying threat.

Jagger had personally upgraded the motorcycles to

make them the fastest things on the street. He'd also equipped them with a specialized magnetic panel where they could rest a weapon without fear of losing it. The feature enabled the drivers to confidently discharge a gun, knowing they could they secure it within two seconds and reclaim a two-handed grip on the handlebars.

This eliminated the need to have an extra person on the bike—one to drive and one to shoot—allowing faster performance and improved agility on the road. He'd done fine work on those motorcycles. Now that they'd been unleashed against him, he realized he'd probably done too good a job, but they weren't indestructible. He'd left a couple of easily overlooked vulnerabilities that he'd exploit.

"Are they the Brethren's mobile unit?" Wendy asked.

"Unfortunately, yes, but only part of the unit." The others were in the tactical vehicle making a beeline to provide backup.

Both motorcycle drivers hesitated, almost certainly catching sight of them and reporting back. Their engines revved and they started weaving around cars, circumventing the stalled traffic.

Jagger grabbed Wendy's hand and took off running around the Mustang.

"We'll never make it on foot through the tunnel," Wendy said.

She was right.

"And we can't stay here either," he added.

They bolted for the entrance. The sound of the motorcycle engines grew louder.

Jagger glanced over his shoulder.

The drivers were easing their way past the stuck cars. The lanes were wide enough, and their motorcycles were so streamlined that they were able to squeak through, even with the metal dividers.

Bullets pinged behind them, ricocheting off the raised trunk door.

Wendy screamed. She let go of his hand and covered her head as they ran.

Jagger drew his weapon and returned fire. "Keep going without me." He dropped the bag on the ground, knelt and unzipped it.

"What?" Wendy stopped dead in her tracks. "Go without you?"

"Don't think. Trust me. Run! Now!"

She looked as if she wanted to argue, but she turned and ran for the tunnel.

The click-clack of her shoes receded in the distance as Jagger grabbed the M18, pulled the pin from the smoke grenade and tossed it toward the Mustang.

He snatched another from the bag and did it again.

Thick layers of white phosphorous bloomed. That might slow the riders down, provide enough conceal-ment for Jagger to pull a Hail Mary and get Wendy out of this alive.

Jumping up, he hoisted the bag on his shoulder.

She was almost inside the tunnel. With the gap in traf-fic, the lane was wide open. Once the Brethren made it by the traffic clogging the road behind them, they'd be able to run him and Wendy down.

Jagger fought to keep his fear for Wendy under tight rein, but his hand was shaking. He shoved emotion away. If he was going to save her, he had to stay focused. He bolted toward the tunnel, his pulse thrumming in his temple.

A motorcycle drew nearer, the rumble of the engine

growing louder. Jagger couldn't see it, yet, because of the smoke, but he sensed it, felt the power of the thrumming motor, though that could have been his adrenaline pumping.

He kept running. Risked another glance behind him.

One of the bikers roared through the smoke, down the lane after them and lifted his gun with an attached suppressor, taking aim.

Heart racing, Jagger raised his weapon and trained his sights at the same time. He fired once, dropping the rider in his tracks, and sent him tumbling across the pavement. But not before a second shot whispered through the air and a searing hot bullet ripped into Jagger's body.

Chapter Five

Wendy's breath punched from her lips. She sprinted as fast as her three-inch Louboutins and long dress allowed. She dodged and changed direction in an attempt to avoid flying bullets that hadn't been fired yet.

I can do this. I have to.

Don't think.

Run!

But her thoughts pounded in her head like her heels against the asphalt. An underground tube that ran almost a hundred feet below the Hudson River was not her idea of safety. Rushing toward it challenged her sense of self-preservation. The closer she got, the stronger the urge to turn back, to avoid the dimly lit confines. Her fear nearly undid her, but Jagger was counting on her not to fall to pieces.

Wendy ducked inside the tunnel and stopped.

She turned around to check on Jagger, make sure he was all right and catch her breath.

One motorcycle rider was down on the ground, but she could hear the engine of the second.

Jagger raced toward her with one hand gripping the strap of the heavy bag on his shoulder and the other, holding the gun, was pressed to his side.

Was he hurt?

If he was injured, there was no indication of it on his face or in his hard-charging pace as he rushed flat out into the tunnel.

Before she could say anything to him, he leaped in front of a sedan in the adjacent lane of slow-moving traffic with his gun raised and stopped the car. "Unlock the doors!"

The driver, an older man in his late sixties, raised a hand in compliance and unlocked the doors.

"Wendy! Get inside." He motioned to her with a hand.

She hurried to the driver's side and hopped into the back seat, leaving the door open for Jagger.

He shifted around the car, keeping the gun pointed at the driver, and slipped inside. "Go! Drive!"

A red stain on Jagger's white shirt spread, blooming wide over his right side. He was bleeding.

She went cold with fear. *Oh, God.* He'd been shot.

"I don't think you want to do this, son," the driver said in a soft, steady voice, but the stony expression on his face gave the words bite.

"You're right. I don't," Jagger said, "but we don't have a choice. Drive."

"A person always has a choice. As both a former United States Marine and a retired cop, I'm telling you that you're making the wrong one. Someone is calling the cops as we speak. They'll have officers waiting on the New Jersey side."

"And I'm telling you that if you don't start driving, cops on the other side will be the least of worries and you're going to have two corpses in your back seat. There's a high probability that you'll be killed, too." Jagger turned and flicked a glance through the rear windshield.

"If you're in some kind of danger, then you need to drop your weapon and call 911," the driver said. "I'll wait with you until the police arrive."

The older man with salt-and-pepper hair was tough as nails, but there was also something tender and kind about him. "Please, sir. Help us. This is a matter of life and death," she pleaded, but he looked skeptical and unmoved.

There was a growing gap between the stationary car they were in and the vehicles transiting the tunnel farther ahead. That alone would draw attention to the Buick if they ever got moving.

"I could put this gun to your head and force you, but I'm asking." Jagger's full attention snapped forward. He undid the shirt button along his wrist, yanked the sleeve up and flashed the driver the tattoo on his forearm—a shield with a lightning bolt across the center. "As one former Ranger to a Devil Dog, I assure you we don't have time for this. Los Chacales cartel is about to storm the tunnel to kill this innocent woman who has done nothing to warrant it. They'll be here any second. Do you really think dialing 911 is going to make a difference?"

The driver raised his scruffy eyebrows at that. "Los Chacales," he echoed, concern entering his voice. "Why didn't you say that from the get-go?" He hit the gas and the silver Buick jolted forward.

A motorcycle zipped out of the smoke. The driver rolled by the cars in line behind them, peering into the window, searching for them. They both scooted down in the back seat.

The older man exceeded the speed limit, trying to

catch up to the traffic in their lane, but if he went much faster, it would draw attention.

The inside of the car was dim from the lack of moonlight and the dull fluorescent lighting of the passageway. The grungy walls of the tunnel closed in and the ceiling seemed to press down, as the length of the underground tube elongated.

Tension spiraled in her chest and ballooned, filling her lungs and squeezing out the air.

She closed her eyes, tried to stop her mind from spinning before she had a full-blown panic attack.

Jagger grunted in pain. The distinct sound tore her away from her private misery, had her head coming up and her eyes flying open.

She put a hand on his shoulder. "How bad is it?" Taking a deep breath and forcing herself to focus, she lifted his shirt and looked at the wound.

He glanced down at his side where he was bleeding. "I got lucky."

It sure didn't look lucky, but rather than a gaping hole, the wound was more of an ugly gash.

"The bullet only grazed me, passed clean through." Blood trickled liberally down his side and her heart clenched. "Only a superficial flesh wound. Better than catching one between the L2 and L3 vertebrae."

The cocky smile that tugged at his lips was quickly supplanted by a grimace.

He was putting on a brave face for her, which meant that he didn't want her to worry, but she was worried. Not only because he was the one thing standing between her and certain death, but... She wasn't ready to face any of the other reasons yet.

"We need to stop the bleeding," she said. "Disinfect it.

Get it bandaged." Would he need stitches? It wasn't as if they could waltz into a local ER. The doctors would be able to tell the wound was from a gunshot. That would trigger an automatic call to the police.

He knew better than she did about the severity, but in this, she couldn't trust his answers. His injury would be glossed over, his pain left unacknowledged, and he'd muster on like a good solider.

Though he hadn't been on active duty for years, had been fresh out of the army when he met her, once a formidable Special Forces operator, always one. It was the way he was wired. As much as she admired his doggedness, at such times it made her want to shake him in frustration. All she wanted was to help him, keep him from bleeding out in the back seat of a stranger's car in the middle of the damn Lincoln Tunnel.

He gave a curt nod and pulled his shirt down, covering the wound. "Later. It's fine. There's no time. They're coming."

"We should at least apply pressure to it," she said, recalling what she'd learned from watching episodes of *Grey's Anatomy*. She looked around, but they didn't have anything clean to use.

A motorcycle raced up the adjacent lane. The sound of the thunderous engine, amplified in the confined structure, bounced off the walls.

"I can't outmaneuver that Los Chacales rider. Not in this tunnel with those lane dividers," the driver said.

They were pinned, for all intents and purposes. Caught in the wave of traffic, the driver couldn't even slam on the brakes and pull a smooth defensive driving tactic.

The motorcycle roared up alongside them. They had

stayed down, but the windows weren't tinted, and the light was dim, not nonexistent. They weren't invisible.

Gunfire pinged, smacking into the trunk of the Buick. Bullets sparked off the metal lane dividers and ricocheted.

"Get lower." Jagger shoved her head toward the seat.

She ducked down, trying to make herself as small as possible as he dug into the bag of supplies on his lap.

Bullets peppered the rear windshield, splintering it into a web of a thousand cracks. If the glass had been tempered, it would've shattered with the first slug. The only thing holding the windshield together was the laminate in the composite, but it would give under a barrage of more bullets.

She'd learned enough about cars from Jagger during the time they'd lived together to qualify as a mechanic's assistant.

Another volley of measured shots quickly followed, striking with plenty of force, and brought the rear windshield flying into the car in sharp chunks. Jagged pieces of glass stuck to reinforced plastic rained over her.

Wendy swallowed a gasp, wincing from the cuts on her hands, which were covering her head, but she was smart enough to stay low and out of the direct line of fire.

More bullets pinged into the side of the Buick.

The driver was shifting gears when a tire burst with a loud pop. He wrestled the steering wheel and tried to prevent the car from swerving, but the Buick slammed against the lane dividers, scraping the steel posts, and scrubbed along the tiled wall. Metal squealed at an ear-grating pitch. She imagined the sparks from the rim grinding against the asphalt.

The rising roar of the motorcycle combined with the

incoming gunfire stretched her nerves rubber-band tight, pulled taut on the brink of snapping. Given the acoustics of the tunnel and the broken windshield, the shots rang out despite the sound suppressor.

Shivering, Wendy closed her eyes. She quelled the panic. Quelled the fear rising in her throat and tamped it down before she screamed.

"Don't let him hit the gas tank," the older man said. "He's coming up alongside us."

In that instant, she didn't know which would be worse, drowning in the Lincoln Tunnel from a freak leak or being burned alive in a car explosion inside it.

Both were outcomes she wanted to avoid at all costs.

"I know. I've got a bead on him." Jagger drew a double-barreled shotgun from the bag, plucked out a box of ammunition and slid cartridges into the chamber.

Clicking his tongue in a sound of satisfaction that she'd long missed hearing, Jagger drew up the cocked and locked shotgun. He pumped the 12-gauge, rolled down the window and shifted the sawed-off barrel through the opening.

She covered her ears with her hands. Plenty of hunting trips with her brother and father had taught her precisely how loud a gunshot could be at close range from a 9 mm pistol, an automatic rifle and especially a shotgun.

Boom!

Wendy flinched, an uncontrollable reflex from the sound.

"Damn it!" Jagger muttered.

He must have missed. Perhaps the driver had swerved in anticipation.

This time, Jagger waited. With a stoic expression, his body tense and poised, he held the 12-gauge upright.

Once the man on the bike shot at them again, Jagger swung the gun out the window and opened fire.

Boom! Boom!

She sat up and hazarded a glance at the scene unfolding.

The motorcycle wiped out. The bike flipped, bounced— once, twice—and rolled, leaving a trail of steely-gray smoke in its wake.

She exhaled with an instant flash of relief that was short-lived. "Do you think he's dead?" she asked, not worried if the would-be assassin had lost his life. She had other concerns.

"If not, he's hurt too badly to come after us," Jagger said, answering her real question.

Metal from the rim scraped against the pavement, making an earsplitting noise.

"Stop the car," Jagger said.

"What?" the driver asked, looking at both of them in the rearview mirror. "Why? Three more minutes and we'll be through the tunnel."

Jagger shook his head. "Only God knows what will be waiting for us on the other side, and I'm not talking about the police."

The driver's gaze lowered. "Oh. I didn't consider Los Chacales might be over there."

"They've got people everywhere," Jagger said. "One phone call, that's all it takes, and they could have anywhere from two to ten people or a second mobile unit waiting to ambush us out there."

The older man nodded. The car gradually slowed, giving the vehicles behind them time to adjust accordingly without causing any fender benders. "What are you going to do?"

"Wing it." Jagger flashed a fearless grin.

On anyone else the confidence would come across as cocky. On him the self-assured demeanor worked. He handled every problem without losing his cool.

He might be hurting, but he didn't appear close to bleeding out.

"I'm sorry about the damage," Wendy said. "If we manage to survive, I'd be happy to pay for the repairs."

"Don't worry about it. This old-timer has a perfect driving record and excellent insurance."

The Buick came to a full stop and the sound of squealing metal faded, but horns blared behind them.

Quickly Jagger stowed the shotgun back in the bag.

He threw open the car door. "Thank you," he said to the driver. Without waiting for a response, he took her hand and she followed him out of the vehicle.

They scrambled into the empty parallel lane as the Buick crawled off and traffic resumed with a few angry beeps.

Jagger looked around for a second as if he was formulating a plan of action.

Standing in the dead center of the tunnel was ten times worse than passing through in a car at thirty-five miles per hour, a speed that had seemed interminably slow minutes earlier. The creeping, prickling terror that started at the base of her spine and slithered over her mind like a shroud had her in its clutches. Her legs turned leaden. The air grew dense. And those tiled walls separating her from the deluge of the Hudson contracted along with her lungs. She could scarcely breathe.

"Hey," he said, and brushed her cheek with his knuckles. "I will get us out of here," he said, sounding so damn confident despite the fact they didn't have a car, there was nowhere to run, and the cartel was waiting for them on either end of this godforsaken tunnel.

"How?" Her heart thudded hard, her stomach rolling in a sickening wave. "What if you can't?"

"I will. Trust me."

This was Jagger during any kind of emergency. Once she'd sliced her hand open while cooking and was bleeding everywhere. He'd bandaged the wound, kept her hand raised over her head to reduce the flow of blood— something she never would've thought of—and gotten her to ER in record time. Jagger always kept his head, prioritized needs, threats, saw that things were taken care of and nothing fell through the cracks. Acted with such calm certainty it endeared him to her and, truth be told, frightened her a little, too.

"The sooner the better." Her voice was a whisper, but he nodded. It was a miracle he heard her over the din from the traffic.

Jagger headed over to the left-side wall.

She bit the inside of her lip so hard she drew blood. The pinch of pain helped clear her head. Wendy took a deep breath, summoning her strength, and forced her feet to move. Jagger pointed up at the emergency walkway for Port Authority personnel as she came up alongside him.

She hadn't considered it previously. Probably because she'd been too busy spazzing out over entering the tunnel in the first place.

Jagger flung the heavy duffel bag onto the footpath under the railing. Then he jumped, catching hold of the ledge, and hoisted himself onto it.

He grunted, but he quickly swallowed the sound of his discomfort.

Once he was situated on the walkway, he reached down for her.

If there was a way for her to get up without bringing him further pain she would've taken it in a heartbeat, but their options were limited, and time wasn't on their side. She hopped, grabbing hold of both of his hands. Putting her feet on the tiled surface for leverage, she walked up the wall the best she could. Her heels kept slipping, but she was climbing for her life, to survive, and each second put strain on Jagger's wound.

Scrabbling up the subway tiles, she gave it everything she had as he hauled her onto the walkway. She climbed to her hands and knees, found her bearings and stood.

"We can't go back," she said, a bit winded, "and we can't go forward."

"So, we improvise."

The stain of blood on his shirt had spread. All the exertion wasn't doing his injury any good.

"Can we take a minute to stop the bleeding?"

"Not yet." He grabbed the duffel bag and hurried along the walkway at a clipped pace.

She looked back toward Manhattan. Plumes of smoke from the motorcycle wreckage obscured her view of the entrance.

If the rest of the Brethren were as tenacious as Jagger, they'd send in reinforcements at any moment. They could have any number of people amassing to cross the tunnel and come after them. A mental image of that possibility made her shudder.

Please, God, don't let that happen.

Patching up Jagger would have to wait. They had to keep moving.

Wendy lifted the hem of her dress and jogged to catch

up to him, wondering what his plan was. It made no sense to run to the New Jersey side when they could have gotten there faster in the car, and it wasn't as if they could go back the way they had come.

"Here we go." Jagger stopped in front of a door appropriately marked Exit.

"Where do you think it leads?"

He shrugged. "My best guess is to a security office with armed personnel, but I like our chances better with them than the Brethren."

She agreed.

Jagger gave the door a nudge. It was locked.

He held up his arm in front of her. "Stand back."

She shifted behind him.

He aimed his weapon at the lock and fired. The door gave way with a kick from him.

On the other side lay a steep stairwell leading to only God knows where.

With one hand, she pulled her dress taut and ascended the stairs after him.

In some ways, she preferred the narrow stairwell to the tunnel and in others she didn't.

The steps and walls were concrete. A material she'd take over tiles any day to keep her dry and safe from the prospect of drowning. Of course she *knew* there were layers of concrete in the tunnel on the other side of those flimsy porcelain rectangles, but logic never outweighed her fear. Not inside the tunnel anyway. Throw her into any other scenario and she kept her wits about her. It was embarrassing.

The climb was strenuous. Not as grueling as the 354 steps, or twenty stories, inside the Statue of Liberty from the ground to the crown. Jagger had taken her there on their third date. Raced her to the top and rewarded her with their first kiss and a view to die for.

In the stairwell, she was huffing, the dank air sawing in and out of her lungs. She was a runner, in good shape, but doing stairs was a killer workout she avoided. Her burning thighs were the proof.

Her mouth was dry, her throat tight. She kept swallowing, which didn't help. Though she silently cursed her heels, she wasn't going to be a slacker or complain. Not when Jagger had been shot, was carrying a bag that weighed a good fifty pounds and hadn't slowed since they had started this ascent toward the unknown.

Finally they reached the top landing and faced a door.

Wendy rested her hands on her knees and raked in oxygen.

Jagger dug back into his bag of tricks. "I'm going to need you to open the door on my mark and stay down low behind me," he said, pulling out the shotgun.

"Anticipating trouble on the other side?" she asked, still a little breathless.

"We've passed three security cameras since we entered this stairwell," he said, but she'd been none the wiser because her head had been down on the climb up. "I didn't want to say earlier, but you're right about the tunnels being a security risk for the city. They're heavily monitored with surveillance." He double-checked that the shotgun was loaded and stood in front the door, poised for action. "I fully expect an armed greeting."

Chapter Six

Drawing in a deep, steady breath, Jagger prepared to handle whatever was waiting for them on the other side of the door.

The use of lethal force would be a last resort with law enforcement. Most cops weren't the bad guys and were only doing their jobs. He had to treat each one like a combatant who didn't know he was friendly.

Jagger nodded his head once, giving Wendy the signal, and she yanked the door open.

"Freeze!" said an armed Port Authority police officer standing in a hallway. "Drop your weapon and put your hands in the air!"

The officer was standing too close. A good thing for Jagger, but bad for her. If she had been two feet farther back, he would've had no choice but to comply or take his chances with her opening fire.

Her proximity gave him a third option.

Rushing forward two steps, he turned the shotgun sideways. He thrust the long barrel up, knocking the officer's gun and sending the muzzle toward the ceiling. He stepped into her and shoved the shotgun again, catching her arms and chin.

Her head flew backward from the force, and her arms

flailed as the gun clattered to the floor. Momentarily shocked, she stumbled back.

Jagger swooped in and seized the advantage, pushing the officer's face forward against the wall. He pressed the barrel into her spine, with his finger off the trigger, and kept her pinned. "Wen!"

Wendy peeked out, taking in everything. She jumped up from behind the door and hustled into the hall. She grabbed the officer's weapon from the floor without him prompting her, and she stuffed it into the duffel bag.

"Zip ties," he said. "Right pocket. Restrain her."

With shaking hands, Wendy took a zip tie and slipped it around the officer's wrists.

Jagger glanced down and checked it. "Make it tighter."

Wendy adjusted it until the officer grunted. Jagger didn't want the Port Authority cop to be in pain, but he also didn't want her getting loose before they made it out of the tunnel.

"How many others in the security office?" he asked.

"Just me. My partner left early."

That was convenient, and if it was true, he wasn't going to look a gift horse in the mouth. "Why did he leave?"

"It's his wife's birthday," she said. "He couldn't get off work, so I told him I'd cover for him."

Jagger took her by the back of the shirt and hurried down the hall, keeping her in front of him. "What time is shift change?" When she didn't immediately respond, he nudged her with the barrel. "What time?"

"In an hour."

Stopping at the small office, he visually cleared each corner before they went in. Jagger steered the officer around the desk and ensured no one was hiding behind it. The office was empty, as she'd said.

Monitors showed various parts of the tunnel, the stairwell they'd come up and a couple of other hallways.

A third Brethren motorcycle had entered the tunnel, and the driver was helping the injured man who had wiped out. They both got on the bike and headed toward the New Jersey side.

Standard protocol. They wanted to clear the crime scene with any surviving members before first responders arrived. No doubt, they'd linger on both sides of the tunnel, watching, waiting for a sign of him or Wendy and a chance to finish their job.

Jagger wasn't going to give them that chance. "When you saw us coming up the stairwell, did you report it?"

The cop shook her head. "No."

Once again, convenient. *Too convenient.*

"I want you to get on comms," Jagger said, "and change the report you made about us." After the gunfire in the tunnel, there was no way she hadn't reported two suspicious individuals heading up the stairwell. "Say we doubled back. That we're on foot in the walkway."

"Going in which direction?" the cop asked.

"West." He shoved her into the chair behind the desk. From her wedding ring, he knew she was married, but he needed more heartstrings to tug. "Do you have kids?"

"Yes. Three girls."

"How old?"

She took a shaky breath but remained calm under pressure. "Seven. Nine. Thirteen."

"I know you want to see your family again. I don't want to hurt you. So while you're on the radio, I want you to remember that I'm armed and dangerous and how much you want to get out of this without catching a bullet."

"Is she your hostage?" the officer asked, referring to Wendy, who was shivering in a corner.

"No. I'm trying to protect her. Save her from Los Chacales hit men. You have no reason to trust me, but on my life, I mean you no harm. I need to get her out of here and I don't have time to debate how that happens."

A single vein popped out on the officer's forehead. He could see her weighing the things he'd told her.

"Okay." She nodded. "Pick up the mic and hit that button," she said, hiking her chin at the one labeled Control Center.

"Play this smart and you'll have a story to share," he warned, just in case she got any bright ideas while on the radio. "A dead wannabe hero tells no tales. Think of your girls." He hit the button, opening the line of communication to the control center.

She licked her lips and sat forward. "Control, this is Morales."

"Morales, what's the status of those two suspects? Are they still headed your way?"

Of course, she had reported it. Any good officer would've, but now he had confirmation and it meant he had to doubt any answers she gave him.

"They doubled back. The woman was having difficulty climbing the stairs. They're on the walkway again, heading west. Over."

"Roger, that. Also, Nichols and Seung are both delayed. Traffic. One of them should be there within the next twenty to thirty minutes."

She'd lied about the shift change, too.

"Good to know," Officer Morales said. "I'll put on a fresh pot of coffee."

"Control, out."

Jagger disconnected and narrowed his eyes at the cop. "You did good, but don't lie to me again."

Wendy came closer and peered at the monitors. Then she flicked a glance at him. In her eyes, he saw she wanted to know what they were going to do.

He was sorting through that. "Where do the other hallways lead?" he asked.

"Two connect with the other tubes," Morales said.

The Lincoln Tunnel consisted of three vehicular tubes with two traffic lanes each. They were currently in the northern tube that had exclusive westbound traffic.

Jagger rifled through the desk for anything he could use. "The other hallways?" he asked, finding a roll of duct tape.

"They lead to topside. One door on the New York end and the other New Jersey."

"Which entrance will those two cops use? Nichols and Seung?"

For a second, her gaze dropped and shifted to the left, but he caught it. Whatever she was going to say next would be another lie.

"New York side," she said.

That meant Jagger and Wendy couldn't go toward New Jersey because that was the real side the other two cops would enter.

"What does topside look like?" Jagger had always wondered where those emergency doors inside the tunnel led. He'd never expected to discover the answer while on the run from the Brethren and now the police.

"It's a parking lot."

"Security?"

She shook her head. "No. The lot is gated."

"Walk me through the procedure to leave."

As she explained, he knew he was getting only the partial truth, but it was better than nothing. He turned to the wall of lockers in the back of the office. Six units.

Inside the first one was a Port Authority Police uniform, black, utilitarian. It seemed small enough to fit Wendy. He snatched the uniform from a hanger and handed tossed it to her. "Change your clothes."

She glanced down at the impractical dress she had on. Looking back up, she nodded, her eyes clear and full of understanding that they needed to blend in. Without saying a word, she unzipped her dress and started changing.

Jagger looked away, turning his back. He'd ached for Wendy for a decade and under different circumstances he might've been tempted to sneak a peek, but in the end, he wasn't the kind of man to steal anything, not even a glimpse.

He moved to the next locker. There was a long-sleeved uniform top that was about his size. He swiped it and dropped the shirt, along with the shotgun, on the desk.

If he didn't get the bleeding from the gunshot wound managed first, he might lose too much blood due to the nature of his injury, risk infection, not to mention that he'd ruin another shirt. Inside the duffel bag, he found the small medical kit he had in case of emergencies. Nothing fancy, it didn't even have tools for a suture.

Jagger set the kit on the desk. Quickly he took off his bloodied shirt and shoved it into his bag. He doused antiseptic on gauze and gritted his teeth in anticipation of what was to come.

"Let me." Wendy was at his side.

She'd changed with the speed of a ninja. The uniform was a little loose on her, but the belt helped. Heels weren't going to work any better than her going barefoot, but one problem at a time.

Holding out her hand, she offered to take over.

He gave her the wet gauze.

She cleaned around the area of his wound. The closer she got to the open gash, the more gently she dabbed, and he appreciated the tenderness.

"I think you're going to need stitches," Wendy said.

"Not a possibility right now." He rummaged in the med kit and fished out the superglue.

"What on earth are we supposed to do with that?" Wendy's gaze flickered from the glue in his hand to his wound. "Are you crazy? I can't." Her voice was strained, sounded thin.

"It's actually not a bad idea to close a superficial wound with it, in a pinch," Officer Morales said. "My husband is an EMT. Seen and done a lot of things. But you should go to the hospital to have that treated."

He should, but Officer Morales hadn't suggested it out of concern.

A trip to the ER for a gunshot wound would be the quickest way for them to be apprehended and for the Brethren to find Wendy.

Needle and thread and a proper suture were his first choice, but it wasn't as if he had many options. He gave Wendy a determined grin.

"You're unbelievable. Stubborn to the core," she said, snatching the glue from him. "This is going to hurt like hell. Are you ready?"

No, which didn't really matter. "Get it done so we can get going."

Wendy squirted the sticky liquid right into his wound and squeezed the skin together.

Jagger sucked in a sharp hiss at the agonizing burn. He groaned through the bloom of pain that lasted for several moments. Then she released the skin and the cut had sealed.

"See. It did the trick." He flashed another grin, though this one was tempered by the sting in his side. "No more bleeding."

"It's not medical grade. The skin could get irritated," Wendy said, inspecting his injury further. "You might get sick or die of toxic poisoning from that stuff."

"Superglue won't kill me. Don't worry, I'm not going anywhere."

Her eyes flashed up at him and her expression changed, turned dark like storm clouds gathering. Something in his words had struck a nerve.

Then he remembered. The last thing he'd said to her in Sing Sing prison.

There is no us. I'm dead to you.

He lowered his head at the sudden tightness in his chest. They needed to talk, have the conversation he'd dreaded since he was released, but right this instant he had only the strength to concentrate on one thing, and it wasn't revisiting that ugly day.

"Thanks for the help. I'll stay on my feet long enough to get you through this," he said to her, recalibrating fast.

Grabbing the clean uniform shirt, he turned away and gathered himself. He threw on the shirt, buttoned it and stared at a Port Authority ball cap at the top of one of the open lockers.

He slipped it on and found another one for Wendy.

"Officer," he said, "we're going to need a few more

things from you, starting with your shoes and your car keys."

While Wendy reluctantly took the officer's tactical boots and put them on, he placed a strip of duct tape across the cop's mouth and used more to secure her torso and legs to the chair.

The communications terminal might still be problematic. Disconnecting the unit would raise a red flag at the control center. For good measure and to play it safe, he wrapped duct tape around the communications terminal. Morales would have to be Houdini to access it.

Checking the time, he estimated they had ten minutes before the officers replacing Morales showed up.

Jagger threw the shotgun in the bag, trading it for the officer's weapon. After taking her holster and placing it on his hip, he stowed the Glock. The badge with a bar code swinging low, clipped to her shirt, was the last item they needed to open the outer door and get through the gated parking lot.

"Come on," he said to Wendy as he was already on the move into the hall.

She was close behind him and then at his side.

He hiked the strap of the duffel bag higher onto his shoulder when they reached the junction of five passageways.

"Which one do we take?" Wendy asked.

The only posted signs were for the connections to the other tubes in the tunnel. The two remaining unmarked corridors didn't indicate which way led west and which east. If they took the wrong one, they'd waste invaluable time and ran the risk of encountering the late officers. Going back to ask Morales meant there was a fifty-fifty chance they'd get a truthful answer, and it was a hundred percent certain it'd eat up time they didn't have to lose. He hoped his naturally strong sense of direction wouldn't falter and lead them astray.

Jagger gestured with his chin toward the left. "If we are dead center along the length of the tunnel, it's about thirty-nine-hundred feet to the exit, give or take." A glance at his watch confirmed they had seven minutes. "Do you still run?"

In high school, she'd been on the track team. A morning run was her thing, rain or shine, during the time they'd been a couple, shacked up in unwedded bliss in a studio apartment the size of a paper bag.

"I've kept it up. Six days a week," she said.

Sundays were for being lazy, making love, breakfast in bed and reading the paper. Not online, but an actual, physical copy of the Sunday *Times*. They always did the crossword together.

Those simple Sunday delights with her—as delicious as their regular daily ones—now belonged to Tripp Langston. That was the way it should be, the natural order of things, but imagining it, knowing it, didn't stop his heart from feeling sick and slow, throbbing like a fish out of water asphyxiating.

"Can you keep you up, injured and hauling that arsenal?" she asked.

"I can handle it." Once a solider, always a soldier. Pushing through the pain came with the territory.

They jogged lightly down the corridor.

He would've killed for a pair of soft-soled tactical boots like the ones on her feet. Once they got to their ultimate destination, there would be a pair waiting. A bigger concern was the possibility of his wound reopening.

Her face took on a hardened edge, her gaze darting

back and forth, searching for danger. The cartel and the cops both posed a threat. They needed to lay low and devise a plan.

They continued jogging in silence until they closed in on a steel door. There was a card reader mounted on the wall with a tiny red light at the top.

He pressed the officer's badge to the card reader. The red light turned green, and the lock on the door disengaged.

They pushed through it and stepped outside.

His skin prickled, though not from the change in temperature. "Damn it to hell." Once again Morales had woven the truth with enough misinformation to catch them up.

Wendy looked at the same thing he was staring at. "This isn't what she described."

Yeah, tell him about it.

Chapter Seven

Hell's bells. The small parking lot was surrounded by a high fence with barbed wire at the top, and at the entrance/exit was a structure the size of toll booth—a manned Port Authority guardhouse.

Wendy ducked back under the overhang of the doorway beside Jagger. "Morales said there wouldn't be security."

"Only fifty percent of what came out of her mouth was true. I think she lied about her replacements coming from the New York side and hedged our bets they're entering from New Jersey, where she hoped we'd be caught."

They were still in Manhattan.

He peeked around the corner at the police officer sitting in the guardhouse. "The cop is facing forward. Maybe I can sneak up on him and immobilize him before he hits the alarm."

That was the first time Jagger hadn't sounded completely confident, like he was capable of conquering the world. Then she tracked his gaze to the reason.

There were cameras mounted on the top of the fence around the perimeter. Most of them pointed outward to detect incoming threats, but a couple of them were trained on the guardhouse and, she presumed, the immediate area surrounding it.

If there were monitors in the guardhouse, the cop might spot Jagger approaching. There was nothing for him to hide behind. The parking spots were set several feet back and only two vehicles were in the lot.

Wendy spotted another detail Morales had given them that happened to be true. Beside the guardhouse was a stand-alone proximity card reader. The badge had to touch the electronic pad to open the gate.

"I think I have a better idea," she said.

"I'm all ears."

She unzipped the duffel and pulled out her purse. Inside, she found the hairpins she'd removed before they left the library. "Morales wore her hair up in a bun. Hers is a little darker than mine," she said, putting her hair in a similar style, "but with the bill of the ball cap pulled down low over my face and it being dark…" She shrugged.

"Might work."

"You'll need to hide in the trunk."

"And you'll need to keep your face turned away and avoid any chitchat with the guard."

"Got it."

"If it doesn't work, for whatever reason, pop the trunk and I'll take care of cop."

What did *take care of* mean?

Jagger hadn't harmed Officer Morales when it would have been easy for him to shoot her. Wendy had to trust his judgment and hope that he wouldn't have to intervene with the guard.

He gave her the car keys and the badge. She stepped out into the lot first. A gust of wind whipped up, nearly snatching the cap off her head, but she caught it in the nick of time.

Holding the ball cap down with one hand, she picked up the pace till she was just short of jogging. She hit the unlock button on the key fob. The lights on a red compact sedan flashed. As the guard's head lifted and he glanced over his shoulder at her, she pressed the button for the trunk. The raised door hid Jagger's approach from plain view and would keep the guard from noticing any differences between her and Morales as she walked.

Wendy stepped behind the open door and waited for Jagger to catch up and climb in.

"You've got this," he said.

Praying that he was right, she gave a nod and slammed the trunk closed.

Her heart raced as she slipped behind the wheel and started the car. The engine turned over right away.

Before pulling out, she adjusted the mirrors. She checked her reflection in the rearview, making sure the bill of the cap was low enough and tucked errant strands back in her loose bun. The hairdo wasn't nearly as tight and tidy as Morales's, but it should pass given the circumstances. She threw the gearshift into Drive.

As she drew closer to the exit, she realized how bright the light was shining in the guardhouse. Even though she and Morales were women with similar builds and hairstyles, the difference between the cop's olive complexion and Wendy's warm ivory skin tone might be noticed if the guard paid attention.

She glanced around the car for anything that might help. A scarf to wrap around her neck. A jacket with a high collar to obscure her face.

In the console, she found a pair of purple gloves. Perfect. They'd hide her French manicure. She tugged them on and got the badge ready to scan.

She eased up beside the guardhouse, tapped the brake and rolled down the window in front of the card reader.

At the same time, the guard turned toward her and opened the sliding partition of the booth that had been keeping the wind out. "Hey, Rochelle."

Without responding, Wendy slid the badge across the card reader. The red light flipped to green and the gate slowly started rolling aside.

"I heard about what happened in your tunnel," the guard said. "Sounded like it was pure mayhem. Crazy night, huh?"

Wendy rubbed her hand across her forehead and temple as if she were exhausted, concealing the side of her face, and nodded. "Mmm-hmm." That was the most she dared utter.

"I heard there was gunfire," he said. "Is that true?"

Her heart pounded out a wild rhythm. "Mmm-hmm." Good grief. Could the gate be any slower?

"I can only imagine how backed up traffic must be."

She gave another nod, keeping one hand up near her face.

Her arm muscles tensed as she gripped the wheel with the other hand.

"Are you all right?" he asked, peering over at her.

"Mmm-hmm." Adrenaline mixed with her anxiety. Staring through the windshield, she watched the gate finally clear the front fender of the car. She waved bye, still holding the badge and pressed the accelerator.

Wendy turned right out of the parking lot onto an unmarked road. Not knowing if there were more cameras in the area, she didn't risk stopping yet and kept her head low.

After a quarter mile, the road intersected with a major street. She put the car in Park at the stop sign and popped the trunk.

Jagger hurried from the rear, around the car to the driver's side, lugging the bag with him.

She had no idea where they were going, but she could follow directions well enough. "You're hurt. You should rest. Let me drive." He was doing too much as it was.

"I'm fine. Save your fight for those who want you dead." Jagger gestured for her to move.

Suppressing a sigh, she climbed over into the passenger's seat. "You're not invincible, you know."

"Yeah, I'm painfully aware of that."

Tension throbbed at the base of her head. He was over-extending himself, putting himself in harm's way for her, and risking everything. She wanted to do whatever she could to help them both, and he wouldn't even let her drive.

"Now what?" she asked, clicking her seat belt in place.

"I considered taking a different tube through the tunnel," he said, turning onto the major street. "The center one will have a travel lane going in each direction, but traffic will be gridlocked anywhere near it now. It'll be a nightmare. We have to use an alternate route."

Fine by her. She never wanted to go through the tunnel in the first place.

Chapter Eight

Emilio Vargas would be in his ocean side villa, sipping on a twenty-five-year-old Scotch, instead of locked up in chains like an animal in the San Diego Central Jail if it weren't for one man.

US Deputy Marshal Horatio Dutch Haas.

Dutch was responsible for this soulless circle of hell Emilio was trapped in. And he didn't mean the hell of being held captive in a jail cell. The hell of wearing an orange jumpsuit with shackles around his wrists and ankles, awaiting transfer to a federal facility. Or the hell of being stripped of his dignity as officers performed a full strip search, including a body-cavity check. An ordeal that would be repeated at the federal detention center.

Prison was nothing. Emilio could handle the invasive physical procedures. Tolerate confinement in a six-by-eight cage. Forgo the extravagances his lifestyle on the outside provided.

He was still king of Los Chacales cartel. Prison wouldn't change that. Not on federal kidnapping charges. The feds couldn't touch his assets. He could rule from anywhere, especially with his son, Miguel, leading their East Coast endeavors as a free man.

For Emilio, hell was losing his daughter.

First, the FBI had meddled in his affairs. The mole they had embedded in his organization would pay for his betrayal, too, no doubt about that. But those pesky marshals went from protecting informants who sought to cripple his empire to crossing the line when they dragged his precious Isabel into the middle of things.

The US Marshals had sent Dutch to get close to Isabel, *seduce* her, persuade her to turn against Emilio. They'd dredged up secrets of the past, and Isabel learned terrible truths he'd never wanted her to know.

All her life, Isabel had grown up thinking she came from a wealthy family who owned legitimate businesses, that Emilio was her *uncle* and Luis was her *father*.

Emilio had had an affair with his brother's wife, something he was not proud of. The illicit relationship had torn the family apart. When Maria got pregnant, Emilio's own wife left him, and Luis suspected the baby wasn't his. Shortly after Isabel was born, Maria had been diagnosed with stage four metastatic cancer. She was gone in a blink. The disease had taken her too damn fast. The day they had buried her, Luis sat him down, told Emilio that Isabel was the last piece of Maria that he had left. He recounted a story from the bible. The judgment of Solomon. Told Emilio that Isabel was his and all would be forgiven between them and they would once again be brothers. Or Luis would cut Isabel in two like the baby in the story and they'd each keep half of her, and then there would be war.

Emilio regretted how he'd wronged his brother, hurt him, and he was no stranger to sacrifice. There was nothing he wouldn't do to protect Isabel. For many years, he'd kept his distance, playing the role of a doting uncle, stolen moments with Isabel when he could, loving her from afar.

He had paid the price for his mistake, for the sake of peace, for as long as he could.

No one had told him that when children were small, they needed their mothers most, but once they blossomed into teenagers, they needed their fathers in a million different ways. The older Isabel got the more she'd needed. More time. More one-on-one attention to feel special and cherished in a manner only a father could give. Emilio had felt that same call to be a part of her life. To be there for her. His only daughter.

War became inevitable, and Emilio had his own brother killed. Not for worldly things, such as money or power. Not to rule the cartel. He did it to be in Isabel's life.

Thanks to the marshals, all his dirty laundry had been aired. He'd been forced into a position where he had to tell Isabel the truth about her parentage, about the family business. Dutch had poured poison in her ear, coerced her to turn on him and had taken her away. Ripped her from Emilio's life like a thief in the night.

Emilio never got the chance to explain his side of things to her. Comfort her from the vicious blows of the truth. To tell her how much he had sacrificed for her, how much he loved her and always would. The marshals even denied him the opportunity to say goodbye.

He risked everything to see Isabel again, went so far as to kidnap another marshal's son for leverage.

I failed once to get vengeance. I won't fail a second time!

That's how the FBI had finally gotten charges on him that would stick. Not because Emilio had been stupid enough to get caught red-handed. The mole had stabbed him in the back.

Special Agent Maximiliano Webb had infiltrated his organization, betrayed him and seen to it that Emilio was charged with a crime that could carry a life sentence.

But it was Dutch Haas, former Delta Force turned marshal, Casanova extraordinaire, who had been hand-picked by the marshals to entice Isabel, charm her, sleep with her, turn her into a traitor.

A slow, simmering rage pumped through Emilio's veins. Still, he kept his face impassive and demeanor apathetic, with the guard on the other side of the bars scrutinizing his every breath.

A reckoning was due, and it was coming. Like a fire-storm, his retribution would be violent and merciless, and nothing would stop it.

For Special Agent Max Webb, Emilio would take his life.

Since Isabel believed she was in love with Dutch, Emilio wouldn't kill him once he found him. Wouldn't hurt a single hair on the young man's head. But Dutch was responsible for taking his daughter away from him, someone Emilio dearly loved. Someone he treasured above all else.

There was a debt and it must be paid.

A life for a life. Emilio would take away someone Dutch cared for.

His men had Wendy Haas in their sights. Dutch's sister was the same age as Isabel. It wasn't coincidence. Emilio had taken it as a sign that it was her life he should claim.

If she wasn't already dead, she would be soon enough.

Wendy Haas wouldn't live to see sunrise. He wanted his men to mess her up before they killed her. Wanted Dutch to live with the idea that she had suffered. Just as Emilio was suffering. He didn't mean the physical torment, though the cops had laid into him last night, not missing their chance to pound out their anger on his body until their captain had stopped it.

No, he was in anguish over Isabel, of what she must think of him, how she must be hurting to have lost two fathers. First, Luis, the man who had raised her, and now him.

Emilio screamed on the inside, seethed from the unfairness of it. He'd done so much, gone to extraordinary lengths—murdered his own brother—to be in Isa's life... and all for what?

If it was the last thing he did, he'd make sure Dutch knew it was Don Emilio Vargas who'd set everything in motion.

Take what is mine and you must pay.

Keys clinked as two officers wearing tactical gear walked down the hall and stopped in front of his cell.

"It's time, Mr. Vargas," Officer Andreas said, unlocking the cell and opening the door. "Let's get this transfer over with."

Emilio stood and shuffled forward to the threshold in his inmate canvas shoes.

Each officer took one of his arms and hauled him down the back corridor. Officer Littleton squeezed harder than necessary on Emilio's arm, making the bruises flare with pain.

Emilio pursed his lips in silent contempt, but he refused to let his discomfort show with even a grimace.

His chains jangled as he plodded along. A throbbing pulse pounded in his temple. His bicep ached under the tightening pressure of Littleton's cruel fingers. His armpits were damp with perspiration.

"Step it up," said Officer Littleton, a big clod of a man, who jerked him forward.

Emilio stumbled and clenched his jaw at the fact that he was at the mercy of the cops to keep him from falling flat on his face.

He loathed being in this position, shackled and herded like a leashed dog.

Littleton punched Emilio's lower back, right in his kidney. The area was already sore and tender from the beating he'd received after being processed. Every blow had been below the neck, each bruise covered by the jumpsuit.

Emilio hissed in pain and his eyes watered, but he didn't cry out. He wouldn't give the cops the perverse satisfaction.

"I said to step it up, not slip up." Littleton snorted.

"Maybe you should back off," Officer Andreas said.

"Why? He's a cop killer and child abductor. This scum deserves it."

It was partially true. Emilio was a cop killer, and he had orchestrated the kidnapping of a child. He was many things, not the least of which was head of the most powerful cartel in the Western Hemisphere, and he wasn't ashamed of any of it.

But he was not scum.

The officers steered him down a flight of metal stairs, and they pushed through a set of double doors that opened into a parking garage. The air was warm and muggy, stifling.

Four additional officers waited beside the armored van along with Captain Kevin Roessler.

Emilio's armed escorts ushered him to the open rear

door of the van, but before they got him inside, Captain Roessler stepped in front of him.

"Good riddance, Vargas," the captain said. "Enjoy your new home."

Music to Emilio's ears. He'd been in that dump of a county jail for almost twenty-four hours and couldn't wait to leave.

It took Andreas, Littleton and two other guards to help Emilio up into the van with the constraints of the manacles. They sat him inside a cramped cage, locked it and took up positions on the bench seats with their weapons at the ready.

The other two must have been behind the wheel and in the passenger's seat in the front part of the van that was sectioned off by a steel plate.

The doors closed and the LED security-recessed lighting popped on. He noted no access to any lock, handle or opening device from the inside of the unit.

Fury tightened his gut over this process, but anticipation of what was to come next had him smiling.

"Hey, what are you smirking at?" Littleton asked. When Emilio didn't respond, the officer slammed the butt of his shotgun against the cage.

That drew Emilio's narrowed gaze.

"You had better wipe that grin off your face," the cop said. "This is no limo service and we're not taking you to a resort for a vacation." He hit the cage again, hard enough to rattle the sides.

"One day you're going to regret having such poor manners," Emilio said around the two soft items hidden in his mouth.

"Oh, yeah?" Littleton sneered at him. Then he hit the cage again. "Can you believe the head of Los Chacales, the freaking *jackals*, is lecturing me on manners?" he asked his colleagues.

Three of the officers laughed.

Littleton was an idiot and lacked respect. He was going to get what he deserved soon enough.

"Let's just get through this peacefully and, I recommend, quietly," Officer Andreas said. He hadn't taken part in the beating last night and was one of the few cops who didn't seem to derive any pleasure from knowing it had happened.

"Yeah, whatever, man," Littleton said, but everyone quieted down.

In the silence, Emilio looked over the guards, took in their bulletproof vests, helmets with face shields, elbow and knee pads, shotguns, rifles, Glocks holstered at their hips.

He smiled again, this time inwardly.

Once the speed of the vehicle increased, he presumed they'd hit the highway. He estimated they were going fifty miles per hour. At this rate, the trip to the federal facility in LA would take three hours.

Fortunately, Emilio had no intention of going to LA. He had other plans.

Plans that were a go. Captain Roessler, one of the men on his payroll, had confirmed it.

Enjoy your new home. The captain had delivered the line with sarcasm, but the choice of words had been positive. If he'd uttered something like *rot in prison*, well, then Emilio would've been expecting a far different outcome.

He closed his eyes, tapping into his other senses. The van was gaining speed. Contained in the rear compartment of the secured vehicle, he wished he was able to see outside.

Music blared in the front, drawing everyone's attention. The officers in the back exchanged confused looks. A minute later static crackled over the speakers, then silence.

Muffled talking between the driver and front passenger. Agitated voices were tinny threads through the steel plate, their speech hurried.

The rectangular window in the steel plate divider slid open. "We've got a problem," the officer in the passenger's seat said.

"What's up?" asked Andreas.

"We're gaining speed, but we're not doing it. The brakes aren't working, either. We can't slow down."

"What?" asked a different officer as he leaned forward. "How can that be?"

"We've got no clue. We tried to radio back to headquarters, but our comms are down."

Littleton let loose a string of profanity.

"That's not possible." Andreas scrubbed his hand on his leg. "Did you try your cell?" He withdrew his from a utility pocket.

"Doesn't work either."

That was because they were being jammed. By the time the officers realized what was happening, it would be too late for them to do anything about it.

"Damn it," the driver said. "I've got no control over the steering wheel now. I can't even exit the highway." He yanked the wheel, and nothing happened.

Panic broke out among the cops. Emilio lowered his head, took a calm, cleansing breath and let a grin sweep across his mouth. The officers were too distracted and frantic to pay any attention to him.

We'll see whose cage gets rattled now. A small laugh escaped him. He couldn't help it. Hell, he didn't want to help it.

"You think this is funny?" Littleton asked.

"Of course he does." Andreas glared at the other cop and threw up his hand in frustration. "He's probably responsible for it."

"What?" Understanding slowly dawned on Littleton's face.

"My phone isn't working either." Andreas shoved his cell back in his pocket as two other officers echoed the same problem.

"No, no. Oh, no!" the driver said.

Wide-eyed with fear, the passenger faced forward, leaving the window in the steel plate open. "Oh, my God!"

The van swerved and hurtled toward a V-shaped concrete barrier. The speed ticked up. They must've been doing at least seventy.

Emilio slowed his breathing and anchored himself in his cage, bracing for impact.

"Try the brakes again," the passenger said.

"I am! Practically slamming my foot through the floor."

The urge to turn his head and look was overpowering, but Emilio didn't want to get whiplash. He did steal a quick glance at the officers in the back sitting on the bench seats. Without seat belts.

Chaotic energy swelled like a balloon about to burst. One officer swore while another started making the sign of the cross over himself. He didn't get to finish.

The van slammed into the barrier. The harsh impact was bone-jarring as metal squealed and crunched. Emilio's teeth chattered in his head. His brain swam. His vision blurred. The world spun round and round in a kaleidoscope of colors and shapes.

He breathed through the disorientation. Shook off the pain. Prepared for the next step—extraction.

His vision cleared. The officers in the back were on the floor, trying to gain their bearings.

Up front, the other two were starting to come to, regaining consciousness. The bulkhead of the vehicle was completely smashed in. They were probably pinned, but still alive thanks to their seat belts and the yellow barrels filled with sand that had cushioned the impact. The heads of both officers up front wobbled. Something drew their attention toward the driver's-side window. They reeled back in alarm. One threw his hands up in the air and shook his head.

Bullets punched through the window in a bright flash of light, making a terrifying sound, and tore into the two officers.

The windows were *bulletproof*, which meant resistant to small arms fire, 9 mm, .357, .45. Whatever his men were using was high caliber and powerful. His guess, a .50 cal machine gun with incendiary armor-piercing ammo.

A buzzing sound started at the back doors.

The remaining officers struggled to recover, groaning and floundering on the floor. They looked like blackbirds with broken wings.

Sparks burst in a swift, fiery arc across the reinforced aluminum of the door. His men were working quickly,

doing their best not to lose their advantage and capital-
ize on momentum.

Emilio didn't know every detail of the plan. It was easy
enough to surmise how his men would proceed based on
experience. He spit out the two foam earplugs into his
hand and stuffed them in his ears. Captain Roessler had
slipped him the hearing protection in his breakfast.

Closing his eyes and turning his head away from the
back door, he covered his ears with his palms, pressing
hard against the plugs to help deaden any sound.

A boom thundered moments later.

Surely, a flash-bang grenade had been thrown through
the hole his men had been cutting. The grenade emitted a
blinding flash of light around six to seven megacandela
and a deafening sound greater than 170 decibels.

A nonlethal device had to be used with Emilio trapped
in the rear along with the cops.

He opened his eyes.

The officers were writhing on the floor, hands clutching their heads, eyes squeezed shut, too late. They couldn't
see or hear and were in intense pain due to the rupture
of their eardrums.

The back doors flew open.

Masked men holding automatic weapons entered. One
made a beeline to his cage. Using a bolt cutter, his guy
didn't waste time searching for keys.

Even with the mask, Emilio knew it was Samuel. A
fierce and loyal lieutenant Emilio had brought up from
Mexico after he was no longer sure who to trust.

Samuel made quick work of cutting the chains of the
manacles and held out a hand to help Emilio up.

Technically, Emilio was a senior citizen, had endured
a vicious beating at the hands of the police and had just

been through a traumatic car accident, but he was no invalid. A hand up wasn't what he needed. "Give me a weapon."

Samuel swung the M4 carbine slung over his shoulder off and passed it to Emilio butt first. The weapon was a shorter, lighter version of the M16A2 assault rifle.

Emilio aimed at his target and pulled the trigger, pumping bullets into Littleton until the man stopped moving. "You dare to put your hands on me!" He needed to expel the words even though the guards couldn't hear him because of the grenade. He pulled the trigger again. "I am the head of Los Chacales!" *You idiot.*

A dead idiot.

As he made his way out of the vehicle, he put a bullet in the legs of the other officers. Except for Andreas. He had shown respect, and for that he would be spared any unnecessary pain.

Two of his men took his arms, propelling him out of the police van and into their own.

The rest climbed in and the side door slid shut.

He glanced at the high-powered rifle mounted on a tripod that had been welded to the floor bed. A .50 Browning machine gun. As he had suspected.

They sped off from the scene.

He anticipated they would soon exit the highway and change vehicles, where fresh clothes would be waiting for him.

"Where do we stand on locating Max?" he asked. His mouth filled with bitterness saying the name. Emilio had trusted Max with his life, and the man had been a rotten, stinking mole.

"I followed him to the FBI building after you were

arrested last night. They flew him out. Chopper on the roof. His FBI handler is good."

"I need him." Not only for revenge, but to send a message to the FBI.

"Our insider at FBI headquarters in Washington, DC, tracked him in the system. He's in Denver, Colorado. Taking personal days."

"Good." Samuel was an excellent lieutenant. The perfect choice to have at his side in a crisis. "Is the Haas woman dead?"

Samuel lowered his head. Never a good sign. "No. She's getting help."

Help? "From whom?"

"I don't know him, but I've been informed." Samuel glanced up with a grave look. "Someone named Jagger Carr."

Shock widened Emilio's eyes, parted his lips. The vein in his neck throbbed painfully. For the first time in his life, he feared getting a ruptured aneurysm.

Hahaha! That was the sound of fate laughing at him. Coming back to bite him where it would hurt the most.

"Is it true, Don Emilio? His father had been your lawyer, your…consigliere? We trained this guy? He's one of ours?"

One of his best.

"Yes." His voice was a whisper and he had to swallow back the bile rising in his throat.

Warren Carr had been a trusted advisor. The talented lawyer had gotten Miguel established in New York City. Had done many unlawful things to protect Emilio's only son from the law as well as other cartels.

In return, Emilio had Jagger trained. To be a warrior. To be formidable. And he was under no obligation to the cartel, the way Warren had wanted it before he'd been killed by a rival cartel in Venezuela.

Jagger had been free to live his own life and even served in the military until he murdered a man and got sent to prison. Inside, he needed Los Chacales for protection, and the cartel was there for him. They had his back. Not only to honor his father's memory, but also Jagger had always been one of them in spirit.

After he was released, he became part owner of one the car shops that did a lot of custom work for them. A natural fit, a welcome one.

Then he had gone to Miguel and asked to be indoctrinated. Jagger had chosen to join the Brethren.

Now he was betraying them. It didn't make any sense.

This was different from Max or Isabel.

Max had been a special agent undercover the entire time.

Isabel never knew about Emilio's dealings with the cartel. She had been sheltered and had no understanding of their code of honor, their ways. What loyalty meant. The price of betrayal.

Whereas Jagger had grown up in their world, had chosen to become one of them, had taken vows when he joined the Brethren.

Emilio didn't want to believe it. Not Jagger Carr!

"I understand there's someone we might use as leverage to flush him out. A sort of stepmother, Tina Jennings."

Warren's old paramour. "She was never Jagger's stepmother. Nothing more than a kept woman. There's bad blood between them. Jagger despises her."

"Why?" Samuel asked.

"Because she stole Jagger's inheritance."

"Miguel is still overseas doing business." Samuel leaned forward, resting his forearms on his thighs. "The *sicario* in New York who has taken the lead on this, Alaric, wants authorization to activate *repo*. What is that?"

Tension snapped through Emilio. "A fail-safe." An acrid taste filled his mouth. Repo was a last-resort measure. Only one or two in the Brethren knew about it and for good reason. If Emilio gave the green light, Alaric and the others would find Jagger and kill him unless... "The boy." Emilio caught himself. That was how he saw Jagger. As a boy, one of his boys. "Jagger wouldn't do this for money." Not honor a blood debt and go against the cartel. "Find his motivation."

"What difference does it make? We've issued kill orders for both him and the woman."

"If I take Jagger Carr's life, I need to know why I'm doing it. I sanction any means necessary to find him, but rescind the kill order on him. Hurt him. Wound him. Cripple him. But spare his life. I want to know why he chose Wendy Haas over me."

Chapter Nine

After navigating the snarl of traffic, it had taken Jagger forty minutes to drive clear across Manhattan and hit the FDR. Not for a single one of those minutes was Wendy able to relax.

Her head was on a constant swivel. The Brethren were out there somewhere hunting them, Jagger was injured, and the car they were in had surely been reported stolen by now.

She didn't want to consider what might happen if the cops pulled them over. They would be arrested. Booked on one, two…too many charges for her to count, and with Jagger's criminal record it would be an utter disaster.

In the end, a repeat of the first time he'd been arrested and railroaded through the system.

Too bad his father hadn't been alive back then. His dad had been a phenomenal lawyer, quite clever from the stories, and he would've done anything to protect his son.

But when Jagger was in the army, deployed overseas, his dad went to Venezuela on business. A travel warning had been issued by the State Department, something about aggression against Americans in the country at the time. His dad was the victim of a carjacking that had gone bad.

She knew that not getting a chance to see his dad one more time, to say goodbye, haunted Jagger.

Wendy wouldn't leave him in the hands of an overworked, underpaid public defender assigned to the case at the last minute. That's how he had gotten such a long sentence before. Wendy had the means now to ensure he'd have proper representation. She wasn't wealthy, but she wasn't hurting either and, more important, she had the right connections.

People owed her favors. A few of them were lawyers.

History wasn't going to repeat itself if she had anything to say about it.

The smooth ride coaxed her to settle back in her seat. Traffic was remarkably light on the FDR Drive at this hour. They were due for a break from the universe. A spot of good luck to cling to.

"We won't be able to stay in a stolen car for long," she said, not wanting to push their luck too far.

"I know. We only need it for another thirty minutes or so."

She glanced out the window at a barge in the water.

"I guess your boyfriend is probably worried sick about you. Sorry you can't call him."

"What boyfriend?" she asked, turning to look at him.

"The one with you at the party. Tripp Langston. Mr. Top Thirty under Thirty in New York City."

Funny enough, she'd forgotten all about Tripp. He was probably curious where she'd ran off to, but Tripp wasn't the worrying kind. If anything, he'd be upset that she hadn't posted another picture of him on her Instagram with the *right* caption and was consoling himself by finding someone to sleep with tonight.

"Tripp isn't my boyfriend."

Jagger's brows drew together. "You're not dating him?" he asked in tone that implied she was lying.

"*Dating* is a strong word, and I most certainly wouldn't use it regarding Tripp." Or any man for that matter. Not since Jagger, and with him, dating hadn't been a strong enough word to describe what they'd been.

It was not only a lack of a relationship since Jagger. She hadn't fully enjoyed sex with anyone, either. He'd ruined her in that way. Every time they'd been intimate, she'd felt a thousand different beautiful things. Desired. Special. Loved. Needed. Cherished. Like she belonged in his arms. In his life.

Being with him had spoiled her, made it impossible for her to climax with another unless she could reach that emotional safety zone, and losing him had made it unbearable for her to risk opening her heart to another. A vicious double-edged sword that kept slicing apart any chance of her being happy with some else.

"We hooked up a couple of times," she said, compelled to clarify for some bizarre reason. Immediately, she was uncomfortable and self-conscious, like she'd admitted to cheating. Which was preposterous.

Things with Jagger had ended ages ago, and he'd been the one to dump her. Freeze her out. Not the other way around.

"It was never anything serious." Why couldn't she shut up and stop talking about it? "We were both going to the gala, thought it'd be bearable if we went together, and it saved me the trouble of booking a car service for the night. Nothing more to it." Not that she owed him any explanation. "And you?" she asked, wanting to get focus off her relationship status. "Is there a girlfriend who is going to wonder what happened to you?"

"No." He was quick to answer.

"No, what? No girlfriend? Or no, she won't worry because you gave her a heads-up you were going to play hero fulfilling some ancient oath you made to my brother?"

He clenched his jaw. "No girlfriend."

She was tempted to ask if he'd dated anyone since he'd gotten out of prison, but it was none of her business and she wasn't sure she wanted to know the answer. He was a healthy guy who'd been locked up a long time. Of course he'd been with someone in the past three years. One plus one equaled two, but she didn't need to hear about it, think about it or visualize details.

Rain started falling. It drummed steady, pounding the car. The rat-a-tat sound mixed with the *whoosh, whoosh* of the windshield wipers, filling the strained silence between them as they headed north. The rain was so heavy it blurred everything else, but she made out Yankee Stadium on the right.

They had gone to a game there once. Another date. She didn't care about baseball, not like football, but the Jets and Giants played at MetLife Stadium in East Rutherford, New Jersey. Baseball had been more convenient.

She didn't recall the score, the snacks they'd eaten, the blistering misery of that Indian summer, the discomfort of the hard seats, the squish of her sneakers as they ran for cover when the sky had opened.

All she remembered was the feel of his arms wrapping around her. Moving into the warmth of his body and clutching his waist. The heady smell of him drawing her closer. How he ran his hand into her hair at the nape of her neck and guided her mouth to his. The brush of his wet lips over hers, a featherlight tease that weakened her knees. The kiss that was so deep and erotic it stole her breath, had heat pooling low in her belly. Left her quivering, aching, needing... She'd wanted him so badly it hurt.

The razor-sharp details sliced through her brain, but it was her heart that bled.

"Do you remember that day?" Putting her head back on the seat, she looked away from the stadium and at him.

Jagger tensed. His knuckles tightened on the steering wheel. His gaze flashed to hers, and in the depths of his stare she saw that he remembered every detail, but he didn't respond right away.

He glanced back at the road. "Which day?"

"The Yankees game. The day I asked you to make love to me." More like begged, believe it or not. She was probably the only seventeen-year-old girl in history who'd had to beg her twenty-one-year-old experienced boyfriend to pretty please take her virginity.

That had been the day he finally made love to her at his place after six months of dating, of kisses and foreplay, sharing themselves, falling deeply, hopelessly in love.

He straightened and stared straight ahead. "I was right. We should've waited," he said. "Given you a chance to date someone your own age. Given you a chance to—"

"Love someone else." Before she was lost to him completely.

He'd warned her. *Once we sleep together, I think that'll be it. For both of us.*

Oh, really. She'd laughed. *Are you that much of a super stud in bed?*

No. I just know you're the one, Wen, and I don't want you to miss out on anything. To have regrets.

"You were wrong," she said.

"About which part?"

She never regretted one moment of being with him. Not one. "I wasn't your average seventeen-year-old."

"No, you weren't."

Her mom had thrown her into kindergarten at four and she'd been placed in the gifted track. Skipped the eighth grade and graduated high school early. Started college at sixteen. "If it hadn't been you, it would have been some other older guy. Some blockhead, probably, who I wouldn't have been in love with. Is that what you wish?"

He was the only man she'd ever trusted with her body and her heart. She'd loved him so much he was a part of her, the other half of her soul.

"I wish," he said, his voice a pained whisper, "that you'd never met me."

The idea was a sledgehammer to her chest, robbing her of the ability to speak for a minute. "If I'd never met you, I'd be dead." It was true, but she wasn't talking about tonight and the cartel.

She'd finished her Crisis Communication and Reputation Management class at NYU and was waiting for the F train. Earbuds in, listening to music, she was absorbed in her instructor's notes on one of her papers. A fight broke out between two guys. She'd been oblivious and hadn't noticed until one guy bumped into her, sent her pages flying up in the air, and her sailing toward the edge of the platform right as the train was coming.

Jagger had caught her, kept her from falling. As if saving her life hadn't been enough, he'd helped her gather up what was left of her paper that had been strewn across the platform. She bought him a thank-you lunch, and over the absolute best falafel she was hit by that thunderbolt—a tug of attraction stronger than gravity. Or maybe it had happened the moment they made eye contact.

"Perhaps that's the way it should be," she said. "Me dead and you free to live your life." She didn't mean it in a pathetic *poor me* way, only as a matter of fact.

"Don't ever say that," Jagger snapped. He turned off the freeway and drove through a town.

The rain came down harder if that was possible. She looked outside at the torrent. Considered everything that had happened between them and how they'd gotten there.

The crushing weight of guilt settled in her chest. If he had never met *her*, he'd be better off. Never would've gone to prison. Never would've gotten caught up with the cartel. Sure as hell wouldn't be on their hit list. He'd be happy, safe, might even be married with a kid or two.

Jagger drove down a dark unpaved path through a stretch of woods and parked. There was a house or a cabin in front of them "We're here."

She didn't even care where *here* was. "I'm bad news for you. Not the other way around. I ruined your life, and I'm doing it all over again."

"What's happening now isn't your fault."

But what happened ten years ago was. "You can't keep saving me. It's going to cost you your life one of these days."

"If it does, then it does."

She clasped his arm. "You have to know when to cut your losses on a bad bet. I'm not worth it."

"Something bad brought us together. Something worse separated us. Now this, but it's not your fault. And I'm never going to sit back and let someone hurt you."

"Because of some stupid promise you made to my brother?" Dutch had taken the vow to heart, seen how much Jagger loved her and pleaded with their mom to back off. But she hadn't, thinking their relationship was too intense, too all-consuming for someone Wendy's age. So, a month after Wendy's eighteenth birthday, two weeks before Christmas, she moved out of the dorms and in with Jagger, and her mother's fears became radioactive.

"No," Jagger said, "not because of your brother."

"Then why?"

He lowered his head. "I guess I can't help myself when it comes to you."

"Even though you hate me?"

His eyes cut to hers, and he fixed her with a fiery stare that made her belly curl and the insides of her thighs tingle. The next thing she knew, his fingers were tangling in her hair and he brought her mouth to his.

She put her hands to his chest in a kneejerk reaction to push him away, but a heartbeat later when his tongue slid between her lips and stroked deep, caressing hers, she tasted him. It filled her up, rendering her unable to think straight, and she found herself pulling him closer. Kissing him back. Her hands slid up his chest and her fingers curled tight into his shirt. It was like some dam inside her that had been holding back years of desire and need broke in a hot rush, and a surge of sensation flooded her body.

His arm locked around her, bringing her against the hard, rugged lines of the one man she'd never stopped wanting. Craving. She wanted to keep touching him, holding him. She wanted to kiss him for hours, the way they used to.

He moaned in her mouth, abruptly drew back, letting her go, and stared at her. "I don't hate you, Wendy. I never could."

That bombshell unhinged her jaw and had her reeling back in confusion.

Jagger reached into the back seat and grabbed the duffel bag. "Let's get inside," he said, the gravelly heat of his voice scraping low in her belly. Then he jumped out into the pouring rain and shut the door.

A million different clashing thoughts rioted in her head as traitorous tears filled her eyes. Jagger had said the words she'd imagined hearing, dreamed of him whispering to her countless nights, but instead of relief, it felt as if a colony of fire ants were under her skin, biting and stinging, full of venom.

Chapter Ten

Inside the cabin, the air was heavy and stale. He lit the kindling and tinder that he'd placed between a few logs. The fire started with ease in the wood-burning stove that was set back against the wall and situated between the living room and eat-in kitchen.

Why did I kiss her?

So stupid.

But man, that kiss…such a tame word for what that had been.

Heat slid through Jagger as he replayed it in his head, making him ache.

Her lips had been so soft against his, and the little sound of pleasure she'd made as he swept his tongue against hers echoed in his ears. He'd savored every delicious second until he broke away. The urge to hold her and do it again was strong. So strong that he knew if he went back outside to haul Wendy in from the car, his mouth would be on hers before they made it to the porch. The rain be damned.

Their chemistry was still there in a big way. Touching her had ignited more than sparks or a brushfire—it was napalm in his veins.

A string of curses churned in his mind.

Jagger welcomed the mounting heat as he shivered from the breeze through the open front door and his wet clothes. When the car door slammed shut, he turned his head in the direction of the sound, but he stayed kneeling by the fire with his hands up in front of the glass door.

Minutes had bled from one into the other while Wendy had sat in the sedan for what felt like forever. She ran up the porch steps and stood on the threshold, drenched, her chest heaving. A shell-shocked look was stamped on her face, as if they'd just escaped another near-death encounter with the Brethren.

"Come in. Close the door," he said softly.

For a moment, he wondered if she'd heard him over the pounding rain because she just stood still, staring at him. Finally, she stepped inside. Shut the door. Locked it.

"There's electricity," he said, "but I'd prefer to keep the lights off tonight."

Houses weren't packed in on top of each other in the wooded area, but they were close enough to see lights on, and he didn't want to draw unnecessary attention. After being released from prison, he visited the place a few times a year to chop firewood and make sure no critters had gotten in. Since he knew the neighbors, he also made the rounds for a quick chitchat.

Sometimes he started the wood-burning stove and lingered, remembering, thinking.

"I've got the fire going," he said. Which was obvious. "You should warm up."

In the amber glow of the firelight, she looked around the living room. Recognition dawned in her eyes.

This was his maternal grandmother's old place in Mount Pleasant overlooking the Hudson Valley. No one knew about the place, except for Wendy.

He had brought her here to escape the city whenever she was out of school and they could both take a couple days off. A two-bedroom, one-and-a-half-bath cabin, surrounded by hiking trails. They'd had a great time here, almost magical. If plain, simple happiness was magic. They always had fun together, regardless of the location or what they were doing. Washing the dishes with her had been fun. They hadn't been a perfect couple. Sometimes they'd argued, but the fighting never lasted long. Never outweighed the laughs, the love, the intimacy—and he didn't mean sex, though that had been sensational, too.

Wendy's gaze narrowed and swung to him.

He wasn't sure if she was upset over what he'd said in the car or that he'd chosen their former love nest outside of the city as a hideout. Maybe it was both.

"Jagger—"

"If you're angry, I understand."

"If?" The misery in her voice caused dread to flash through him.

She had a right to be angry and hurt, and he'd face it. Answer for the choice he'd made.

Nonetheless, his throat tightened. "We'll talk." He stood and eased toward her. "Let's get out of these wet clothes first. Dry off. Change. I'll make us some tea. Okay. I didn't go through all the trouble of getting you away from the cartel only to let pneumonia do you in." He wiped rainwater from his face. "You still have some things here. Upstairs in the bedroom." It had been easier to keep basics here and not worry about lugging a bunch of stuff back and forth. "I couldn't bring myself to get rid of it."

"You could've mailed me my stuff since you knew

my address before tonight." Accusation knifed through her tone. "Didn't you?"

Guilty as charged.

What he'd meant was, he didn't *want* to get rid of her stuff. He still buried his face in her soft, delicate night-gown, even though it didn't smell like her anymore. That was one of the things he missed. Her smell. Her smile. He could go on and on. "Yes. I've known for a while."

A tremor ran across her face. She clenched her hands into fists, as though she might sock him in the jaw. He wouldn't blame her if she hit him. Hell, he deserved it, and if memory served, she had a solid right hook. He admired her strength and grit, but the hurt in her eyes was gutting him. It was a sharp reminder that although she was strong, she was vulnerable, too.

He lowered his head.

All the things he'd longed to share with her since his release bombarded his mind, but he didn't want to be selfish. Doing the right thing wasn't easy. He needed to measure his words before they left his mouth.

He took the flashlight from the kitchen table, switched it on and climbed the stairs quickly, taking them two at a time. Behind him there was silence. She hadn't moved. After a minute, there was the creak of floorboards in the living room, something rustled, and then the old wood stairs groaned as she came up.

Moonlight spilled in through the large window at the end of the narrow hall.

He entered the first cozy bedroom, the one they'd once shared. "Your stuff is in there." He gestured to the closet.

She stepped inside the room with her glittery purse under her arm and Corey's 9 mm with the attached silencer in her hand.

"Planning to shoot me?" he asked, half-joking.

"Not tonight," she said, her voice devoid of humor. She turned, facing him with a neutral expression. "I didn't want to be up here, getting changed, alone, without protection. Just in case." She shrugged.

He nodded. Things were calm, but emotions were running high. The adrenaline kick from earlier still had his heart pumping hard—or it could've been from kissing Wendy.

The need to be prepared for the unexpected was familiar. That was the only reason he'd kept the electricity going. He didn't come out here often enough to warrant it, but he had an alarm system installed, and sensors on the road leading up to the house and at various intervals around the house throughout the surrounding woods. Her having a gun was a good idea. She knew how to handle a firearm, but until now she hadn't seemed calm enough to use one.

Jagger handed her the flashlight.

She took it and walked to the closet.

While she looked around at the things hanging up and what he'd packed in a box on the floor, he grabbed a change of clothes from the dresser, along with a pair of dry socks.

On his way out of the room, he snatched his worn-in hiking boots. They weren't tactical, but they were ten times better than the soaked dress shoes on his feet.

"Take your time," he said, wanting her to decompress a bit. He knew better than to have a conversation with her when she was fire-spitting mad at him. "There should be plenty of hot water if you want to shower, but you'll need to let it run a minute or two."

"I remember." She kept her back to him as she fingered through clothes hanging in the closet.

"Do you want chamomile tea?"

"Earl Grey. I don't see myself settling anytime soon."

Neither did he, on edge and feeling he was missing some important detail. "Powdered creamer?"

"Yes, please, and a splash of bourbon if you've got any."

He did. A bottle of Buffalo Trace in the kitchen cabinet. "Sure." He hurried out of the room, shutting the door. Putting a little distance between himself and Wendy while she undressed was probably a good idea.

In the tight hallway bathroom, he grabbed a towel. Everything up at the cabin was old and comfortable. It reminded him of his grandmother. His mom had died from a hemorrhage while delivering him. With modern medicine and technology, you wouldn't think women in developed countries died during childbirth anymore, but it was alarming how many did.

His grandmother had filled in, helped his dad raise him. She'd bequeathed him the cabin and her jewelry. He'd forever be grateful to her for being the warm, maternal influence that he needed in his life. Taught him how to be tough yet tender. Patient. That sometimes you had to sacrifice for the ones you loved.

Downstairs, he put the kettle on for tea and set the bottle of bourbon on the kitchen table along with two mugs.

The rain was letting up, shifting from a downpour to a drizzle.

He set the alarm. On the security panel, the ten sensors around the property and on the path up to the house were a row of bright green dots. He undressed near the fire and toweled off.

The stairs creaked as he finished putting on his pants and socks, but he hadn't pulled on a shirt yet.

"That was fast," he said to her, shoving on his boots.

"I couldn't relax enough to take a shower." She walked over wearing a pair of jeans, a light blue long-sleeved pullover that clung to her curves and a pair of Keds. "Everything sort of fits." She gestured to her clothes. "Albeit somewhat tightly."

She wasn't as lean as she had been as a teenager. Her body was softer, sexier. No longer a pretty girl, she was a stunning woman.

"You look great," he said.

Wendy's gaze dropped from his face to his bare chest. She grimaced and closed the space separating them. "When did you get this?" she asked, tracing the lines of the dagger tattoo over his heart.

Her touch on his bare skin sent a flush of warmth through his entire body. She had him spinning, fantasizing about things he couldn't have.

Focus. "Got it as part of initiation into the Brethren."

"Why did you join the cartel?" Her fingertips lingered on the raised skin in the center of the hilt of the dagger. A permanent mark of the Brethren. An oblong scar, a brand that, unlike a tattoo, no laser could remove.

He turned her face back to his. "In prison, I needed protection. It was a brutal world behind bars. Push came to shove, and the safety of a group became essential to survive."

His mother had been a WASP with blond hair and green eyes, and Jagger favored her more than his Latino father in looks. In jail, his choices had been the white supremacists or the cartel. He was proud of his Hispanic heritage and didn't want to hide it.

Los Chacales were many horrible, questionable things, but at least they weren't racist, and he knew their world. Grew up in it. His father had been a part of it. Why or how his dad had first gotten involved with Emilio Vargas, Jagger would never know. But he would take a dagger over a swastika any day.

"Needing protection, I can understand." She dropped her hand, and he missed the heat of her hand. "But joining the Brethren? Choosing to become an assassin? I don't understand. That doesn't sound like the Jagger I used to know."

Didn't it? He'd killed for Uncle Sam. He'd killed for Wendy. But it was true that he'd never wanted to take the life of another. "It's complicated. I had my reasons."

The kettle whistled. He grabbed a pot holder and removed it from the stove. After making her tea, he opted for two fingers of bourbon neat.

He yanked on a T-shirt and put a button-down over it, leaving the shirt open.

They sat on the area rug in front of the fire, each holding their respective mugs.

She blew on her tea and took a timid sip. "There's a lot I don't get. In the car…" She looked up at him. "If you never hated me, then why did you send me that horrible letter and say those terrible things to me on my last visit to the prison."

Taking a healthy gulp of bourbon, he aligned his thoughts. To make her understand, he had to start from the beginning. "That night you had to work late and close the restaurant."

"The night that ruined us," she said, shaking her head. "I should've quit when you asked me to. Never should've flirted with customers for bigger tips like the other girls."

After Wendy had moved in with him, her mom had cut her off, stopped sending checks to pay for tuition. So Wendy, being headstrong and just as determined as her mom, didn't go back to the dorm, and instead got a job. At a restaurant called Bazooms. She became one of their *girls* and had to wear a revealing outfit, skimpy shorts that barely covered her bottom and an unforgiving tight tank top. A smile and a wink at the mostly male patrons meant bigger tips, and he'd never faulted her for that. Sometimes, though, the guys got drunk and handsy. Wendy was a looker, and he wanted her to be careful.

Any time she had to close the restaurant, he swung by and walked her home.

That particular night, he'd been late picking her up, and she had taken out the trash alone. By the time he arrived, he found her in the alley adjacent to the restaurant. Two guys had her cornered behind the dumpster. One had a broken beer bottle to her throat.

Jagger had gotten there before anything had happened to her, but he'd seen red and lost it. His control had slipped for a moment, a heartbeat, and he'd killed the man with the bottle.

"What happened wasn't your fault." Jagger set down the mug and caressed her face.

At that, one of her eyebrows rose and she pulled back from him. "You wrote me a Dear Wendy letter stating the opposite. I still have it. Memorized every ugly word. I told myself that if you saw me, you'd take it back. Tell me you didn't mean it. But you didn't, did you?"

Separated by a plexiglass partition, he'd looked her in the eye and yearning, startling in its intensity, had clawed at him. All he'd wanted was to hold her, reassure her that he'd never stop loving her. Instead, he'd picked up the intercom phone and told her how much he hated being behind bars. How much he hated *her* since she was the reason he was locked up.

He'd make the same choice, utter the same words if given the chance for a do-over.

"Wen, you're so stubborn." She would've kept visiting twice a month, holding on to their relationship, living half a life and enjoying none of it. That was the last thing he wanted, and when her mom came to see him and begged him to put an end to it, he'd known what he had to do. "It was the only way to get you to walk away from me."

Not that any of his sacrifices had prevented her, him and death from colliding tonight. Now he'd attacked fellow Brethren and he was diving back down the dark rabbit hole he'd never truly escaped.

Wendy set down her mug, and her blue eyes found his. They were so pale in color, almost icy yet somehow also warm and vibrant. "*You* were my life, Jagger. I would've waited for you, forever."

He knew it. "That was the problem, honey. You were only eighteen." Not that it would've made a difference if she'd been twenty-eight or thirty-eight. He was facing a fifteen-year sentence. "I didn't want you wasting your life waiting on a murderer to get out of jail. I promised Dutch and your mom that I would always look out for you." Even if it meant that he had to cut out his own heart and smash it into a million pieces. There wasn't anything he wouldn't do for Wendy. "You deserved better. More. To be able to move on from a convicted felon. To be happy."

"Move on? God, Jagger, do you really think there was ever any moving on from you?"

"Yeah, I do. You're successful. Dating lawyers, businessmen, doctors, that stockbroker, the Orca of Wall Street."

"Lawyers? Doctors? You've kept tabs on me?"

Jagger heaved a weary breath. Getting sidetracked wouldn't be helpful. "My point is you did it. I pushed you away so you could have it all—success, a relationship— and you do."

"Are you kidding me? I don't have happiness. And I haven't *dated* anyone since you. With all the walls I've built around myself so that no one would ever hurt me that badly again, I've never gotten close to another man."

"But on Instagram and the magazine—"

"It's all fake. Appearances. I've been with other people, but anyone else was a distraction. Every morning when I wake up and every night when I go to bed, *alone*, all I feel is empty." Tears filled her eyes. "We had everything together. What most people dream about, go their whole lives craving, and never find. Someone we loved so much we would die for them. Kill to protect them. You weren't a murderer to me. You were my soul mate. You were my heart. My everything. When I lost you, I lost a part of myself, too."

Mrs. Haas had cried, yanked on every heartstring he had. Demanded he prove how much he loved Wendy by letting her go.

Breaking up with her while he was in prison, telling her that he blamed her, hated her, had been the hardest thing in the world for him. He'd thought she'd heal, move one, forget about him. The selfless thing to do was to set her free. Wasn't it?

"Wendy, I didn't know." He cupped her face.

Sorrow passed across her eyes like storm clouds.

"What's so awful is that you weren't honest. All this time I thought you blamed me, hated me for what happened."

If he had been honest, she never would've left him. "It wasn't your fault."

"You let me believe that it was. Do you have any idea how that guilt has eaten away at me? Changed me? I was devastated." Her voice broke, and so did his heart.

"I never thought you'd believe me." He loved her so completely he wasn't sure if their bond could be severed. After he'd sent the letter, he'd known she would visit him. A part of him thought that no matter what he said, she'd feel how strong his love was. That she'd keep coming to visit, but she hadn't. He'd reconsidered, thought about reaching out to her, apologizing. Telling her the truth. But he'd been resigned to do right by her. Even though it had shredded him, he'd forced her to walk away and had to live with it. "I tried hard to sell the lie because I thought it was the right thing to do."

He took her hand, lacing their fingers together.

The rain had stopped, not even the pitter-patter of a drizzle. Silence wrapped around them, and he longed to have those ten years back with her.

"I'm not sure which is worse." Her face was tight with pain. "The lie you told me, or the betrayal of pushing me away like that when we swore to be there for each other?"

Guilt was like a shard of glass in his heart. "I'm so sorry." Pressing his forehead to hers, he stroked the back of her hair. "I'm sorry I lost control." He'd been so angry, seeing that broken bottle at her throat, and everything had unraveled fast. One wrong move and he'd killed that guy. A complete accident. A cruel twist of fate. "I'm sorry for hurting you."

All he'd ever wanted was to love her and make her happy.

Many nights he had lain awake in his cell thinking how different things would've been if she'd never taken the job at Bazooms. If she'd stayed in the dorms. If his dad had left him more than a vintage car and a cryptic letter about legacy while his father's lady friend inherited millions.

Peering into his eyes, she lifted her hand to his cheek, and when she touched him something inside of him came alive. Something he'd tried to bury.

A desperate, soul-deep longing for her to be his again.

"Why didn't you come see me after you got out, instead of stalking me?" she whispered.

Great. She did think of him as a stalker. "Getting released didn't change anything."

As soon as he was out of prison, he'd looked her up, gone to her apartment. Saw what a successful power player she'd become. She'd been dating a lawyer at the time. Not that it had mattered. With her pristine, high-profile image, rubbing elbows with politicians and jet-setters, she didn't need the scandal of associating with an ex-convict. Not even on a casual level and certainly not an intimate one—and that was precisely where any acquaintance would've led.

She rebranded all sorts of people, but there was no making over a murderer any more than putting lipstick on a pig made it attractive.

Trying to pick up where they had left off and recapture the past still would've messed up her life. The paparazzi would have had a field day with it, and she would've lost big clients.

"You were free. That changed everything," she said.

"Unless you fell out of love with me. Didn't want to be with me anymore."

As if that was ever possible.

He leaned in and kissed her, a warm press of his lips against hers. If he could've absorbed her pain and borne it in her stead, he would've without hesitation. He kissed the corner of her mouth, down to her chin, lower to her jaw, and up to her earlobe as she softened against him.

"Wen," he said, low in her ear, hyperaware of her body so close to his, "I've never stopped loving—"

The alarm chirped. They jumped apart and he was on his feet.

"What is it?" she asked.

Another chirp. Jagger cursed himself for dropping his guard.

He moved to the security panel on the wall near the door. Two of the sensors had been tripped and had turned from green to red.

Three more chirps and the lights changed in tandem.

"Damn it. They're here," he said.

Chapter Eleven

Oh, God! Wendy's whole body tightened, and she tried to tamp down the fear that was swamping every inch of her.

"They're on the path that leads up to the house and they're crawling all over the woods," Jagger said.

Wendy scrambled to her feet, her heart already thundering in her chest. "How did they find us?"

"I don't know." He shook his head, throwing her a bewildered glance.

Three more chirps sounded.

"We've got to get out of here." Jagger dug into the duffel bag, pulled out the Port Authority officer's service weapon and tossed it to her.

He looked down her body and his posture stiffened. She followed his wide-eyed gaze to her chest, and her breath caught. A red laser dot wavered over her sternum.

Jagger launched himself at her.

The window shattered. A whisper of bullets whizzed overhead.

With his arms tight around her, they hit the floor. He took the brunt of the fall, but the side of her head smacked against the hardwood. Pain mixed with blinding panic as a groan left her lips.

He rotated, tucking her beneath him.

Bullets slammed into the wall where she'd been standing. The thud on impact reverberated in her chest. The distinct sound bit through the shrieking alarm.

Jagger covered her with his body, protecting her face from the falling glass and flying debris. He rolled her onto her stomach. "We need to get upstairs to the attic. There's another way out." He grabbed the duffel bag and urged her to move.

Without voicing the questions that ricocheted in her mind, she crawled toward the stairs. Using her forearms and knees, she scooted forward with her belly on the floor.

The gunfire was coming from every direction. The cabin must be surrounded.

Jagger shot back through an open window. The crack of gunfire from the shotgun was ten times louder than the sound-suppressed barrage from the weapons targeting them.

Neighbors would hear the ruckus and call the police. Whether that would work for or against them remained to be seen.

"You need to make it upstairs to the attic," Jagger said, "before they get inside."

"Me? What about you?"

"I'll hold them back."

Emotion held her frozen in place. In her head, she knew that not following his instructions wasn't going to help either of them. But, in her heart, she couldn't leave Jagger behind.

For years, she'd been bitter and angry, struggling to recover from the fallout of loving him. She was grateful to have learned the truth. Knowing that he didn't blame her or hate her freed her to be herself. After everything they'd endured, she wasn't going to let him die for her.

They had to survive this together.

"I'm not leaving you." She couldn't bear to lose him a second time.

He glanced at her. Tension stretched across his face and then something changed in his eyes. A split-second decision was made.

Jagger dropped the bag at her feet and duckwalked deeper into the room, carrying the shotgun. When he reached the wood-burning stove, he opened the glass door and, using a fire poker, he knocked out flaming chunks of wood. He lobbed one piece onto the sofa. A second hit a curtain.

No, no. He was burning down his grandmother's cabin.

The smoke and the fire might slow down the Brethren from following them and help conceal their exit, but this was a place Jagger cherished.

Several red lasers cut through the air above his head. Another volley of rounds shattered the rest of the windows, spraying the floor with glass and boring into the furniture. Pieces of wood kicked up near her.

She lowered her head, while keeping Jagger in her sights.

He pivoted and snatched the towel from the back of a chair. Staying low, he crept across the floor to her.

"Take it." He thrust the damp towel at her. "Put it over your mouth and nose."

A man slipped through the broken window closest to them. Jagger spun on his heels only to be greeted by automatic gunfire.

Wendy ducked as Jagger squeezed off two rapid shots from the double-barrel shotgun, putting the intruder down. Just as quickly, another man climbed through a different window.

Jagger redirected the muzzle at the newest threat and pulled the trigger.

Click. The 12-gauge was empty. Jagger lunged for the man with the shotgun raised. He slammed the butt of the gun into the man's face. Once. Twice. Three times. Lightning fast.

Flipping the shotgun in his hands, Jagger gripped it by the barrel like a baseball bat and swung. Metal connected with the man's skull with a loud crack, and he dropped to the floor.

Incoming gunfire forced Jagger to crouch low.

"Here!" Wendy slid the 9 mm in her hand over to him.

He switched off the safety and aimed at the windows. "Get upstairs! I'll be right behind you."

Hot flames consumed the curtains on one window and swept up the wall. Fire licked across the sofa. Smoke suffused the room. The gray air clouded her vision and made her eyes water. But the moist breeze from the open windows sucked out some of the smoke while feeding the flames at the same time.

How much longer would Jagger be able to breathe in there? Smoke inhalation would kill him faster than the fire itself.

Already the smoke burned her throat, and the heat from the flames was mounting. Coughing, she put the towel over her nose and mouth.

Jagger didn't run or duck. He was in full-offense mode. "Go!" He shot controlled bursts of rounds at each window.

She coughed at the irritation in her lungs. The smoke

was getting bad. She grabbed the handles of the duffel bag and dragged it up the stairs, one step at a time.

Two more dark figures slipped through the windows behind Jagger. He spun before she had a chance to warn him, and he pumped bullets into them both, taking each person down with a sickening thud.

The gunshots, the bloodshed, the fire—everything happened in seconds. Heart-clenching, panic-stricken seconds of sheer terror.

She made her way to the top landing with the rest of the weapons. It would save Jagger time, allow him to move unencumbered up the stairs. If only there was more she could do to help him.

Grunting, she tugged the bag across the floor to the bedroom. In the corner on the ceiling was the hatch door to the attic. She jumped up, catching hold of the handle, and opened the door. The pull-down ladder popped out and she unfolded the stairs.

Jagger. Where was he?

She reached into the duffel bag and took out the first weapon she touched. It was a lightweight submachine gun. Her hands were shaking. Fear threatened to overwhelm her and shut down her brain. One thing stopped her from spiraling—the thought of Jagger dying for her. She forced herself to calm down, her focus becoming razor sharp.

Breathe, aim, shoot. She'd been hunting with her family and to the shooting range with Jagger plenty of times. This was the same, she told herself. Except she was the prey going up against a deadly predator. This was do-or-die.

Switching off the gun's trigger safety, she hustled into the narrow hall.

Jagger reached the top of the staircase.

Exhaling in relief, she clutched her chest. He ejected the magazine of the 9 mm. It was out of ammo. He glanced up, shuffling toward her.

Footsteps thundered up the stairs, the old wood groaning from the heavy weight.

Jagger whipped around, shielding her. But his weapon was empty.

A large man bounded to the top step and charged him.

Jagger shoved her aside, sending her stumbling back into the bedroom.

The tall, burly man seized Jagger by his shirt and kept barreling down the hall.

Wendy scrambled out of the bedroom. Raised the gun the gun, her finger on the trigger.

Without a clear shot, she might hit Jagger.

The two men fought, wrestling one another, locked in a deadly tussle. Jagger struggled to break free from the man, who looked strong as an ox.

She aimed low, hoping for an opportunity to hit the man in the leg or foot.

No such luck. The guy didn't stop moving. He pounded forward with gut-churning force, driving Jagger toward the window.

With a vicious grunt, the man picked Jagger up off the floor and bulled him through the windowpane.

The glass shattered as both men plummeted.

No! Her heart nosedived to her stomach.

She dashed down the hall and looked outside. Jagger and the other man rolled on the roof of the wraparound porch, still grappling, and tumbled over the side into the darkness.

Horror rose inside her and washed over everything

for a second. She stood there, a loaded gun in her hand, unable to do anything, and had never felt more powerless in her life. For too long she had been helpless to do anything for Jagger, and now she had to do something. He needed her more than ever.

She couldn't go outside the window after him and the first floor was on fire.

There was only one option.

The attic. Jagger would want her to find the way out.

She whirled to go back to the bedroom. Another dark figure was clearing the top of the stairs.

Without thinking, without hesitation, she lifted the submachine gun, aimed center mass and pulled the trigger. The recoil was stout, but she didn't stop firing until the body dropped.

She ran to the bedroom.

In the closet, she grabbed an old backpack and tore two windbreakers from hangers, stuffing them inside. The duffel was too heavy for her to carry so she threw a few things into the other bag. Ammo, a couple of weapons that'd fit, the small pack of what she assumed was plastic explosives, and her purse.

She shoved her arms through the straps of the backpack and climbed the ladder. In the attic, she pulled the folding staircase up behind her.

What was the plan? Why did Jagger want her in the attic?

Spinning around, she scanned past the sheets of dense insulation for something useful. There was a window that hadn't been there years ago. Jagger must've put it in.

She sidestepped slowly across a ceiling joist, holding her arms out for balance. At the window, she spotted the rigged contraption.

Jagger had installed a zip line.

They'd once had a blast on a zip line adventure tour in the Catskills at Hunter Mountain. The highest, fastest, longest zip line canopy tour in North America.

She opened the window and peered out. Cool, sobering air swept over her, bringing goose bumps to her skin.

The zip line Jagger had set up started at the house. Where did it lead?

Outside, there was only the foreboding darkness of the woods, stretching out in a jagged sea of black. She imagined slamming into branches or, worse, smacking into the side of a tree in the dark.

Trust him.

He had a plan, Mr. Always Prepared. She simply had to put her blind faith in him.

Then something stood out in the distance. A little less than a quarter mile away in a straight line of sight were pinpricks of tiny lights. A neighbor's house?

She slipped her legs through the holes of the harness and adjusted the strap around her hips. Sitting on the window ledge with her feet dangling, she grasped hold of the trolley handles. The smell of burning wood was strong. She saw the smoke, heard the crackling of the fire.

Was Jagger all right?

That tall, burly man was insane to have taken them both through window down two stories. Like someone filled with viciousness and anger and nothing to lose.

Bile rushed up the back of her throat, and she had to fight the urge to throw up. One step at a time, that's how she'd handle this. She blocked out the rest. Refused to allow doubt and worry to paralyze her. First, she had to get safely to the ground.

She released the brake and let the trolley rip.

The roar of the fire drowned out the familiar gritty buzz of the zip line. Sailing through the air, she glanced back.

Flames crawled up the side of the house and danced across the porch, but that's not what sent an icy chill shooting through her heart.

The big guy seized Jagger from behind with a snake-like strike that locked him in a choke hold.

Jagger was in trouble.

Chapter Twelve

Jagger struggled to get a lungful of air. His neck was pinched in the crook of Alaric's right elbow, crowded between the bulge of his bicep and his meaty forearm. The pressure was cutting off the flow of blood to Jagger's carotid artery.

In about thirty seconds, it would put his lights out.

There was one good thing in all this. In his peripheral vision, he caught sight of Wendy zip-lining away from the burning house and into the woods.

She was safe, but not out of danger.

Pivoting, Jagger forced Alaric to move with him, turning their line of sight away from the zip line in case he spotted it in the light from the flames.

His lungs strained for oxygen, feeling like they were going to burst. The heat from the raging fire was blistering. The alarm was screeching.

"Time to take a nap," Alaric growled in his ear over the noise.

And then Jagger would be as good as dead.

He stepped forward with his left foot, stepped back with his right while throwing an elbow into Alaric's solar plexus—knocking the wind out of the guy—and rotated out of the hold.

Still in motion, Jagger reached for Alaric's weapon, but a fist smacked into the side of his face. Surprised, he stumbled back and before he recovered, Alaric was on him.

The man was large and heavy with muscle, but he moved with the speed of a lion.

Alaric drove Jagger back and down to the ground with his thick hands wrapped around his throat. They'd gone from a choke hold to a stranglehold, from bad to worse.

"If it weren't for the old man, I'd snap your neck," Alaric said.

The words rattled through Jagger's head. Don Emilio wanted to spare him? He didn't have time to make sense of why.

He slammed the heels of his palms against Alaric's temples. The striking blow would disorient him.

The guy grunted, and the death grip loosened just enough.

Jagger grabbed Alaric's shoulder with one hand and his forearm with the other in a cross grip. At the same time, he slammed his foot into the Alaric's hip, and rotated, flipping the guy over.

Now they were both down on their backs, perpendicular to each other, but Jagger had his legs around Alaric's throat and the man's arm locked in a game-changing position. Jagger thrust his hips up and he yanked the thick arm backward, breaking the bone.

Alaric roared in pain, but his cry was lost beneath the earsplitting sound of the blaring alarm.

This would've been the perfect time to question Alaric and get much-needed answers that could help them survive. At the top of his long list—how did the Brethren find them?

Jagger had been careful. Taken all the necessary precautions and made certain they weren't followed. This was no fluke, no coincidence, but he couldn't risk taking the time for an interrogation, even a speedy one.

There was no telling how many more *sicarios* were out in the woods or if any had seen Wendy escape. He had to take this win for what it was worth. Temporary, but appreciated.

Jagger snatched Alaric's weapon, jumped to his feet and hightailed it into the darkness.

The stretch of land along the path of the zip line was a thousand feet long and densely wooded, with heavy growth even this early in the year.

When he joined the Brethren, he had decided it would be wise to have a backup plan. A hideout. But it was only safe if he had a contingency in the event the backup failed. He'd installed the alarm and sensors. Cleared a narrow path through the woods, trimming tree limbs where possible and chopping down maple and oak trees when necessary.

The hard preparation was paying off.

Jagger ran down the path, hard, at an all-out sprint. He didn't know if anyone had spotted Wendy fleeing the cabin and pursued her into the woods. Tearing through the night across damp soil and over a stream, he didn't slow for a second. His heart raced, damn near beating out of his chest.

The roar of the fire and the blare of the alarm grew more distant.

Alaric had been in charge. One of the most senior members. Tough. Shrewd. Unrelenting. An excellent choice to have leading the proverbial troops unless you were the target.

Jagger had gotten lucky in more than one way. The roof of the wraparound porch had broken their fall, sparing his spine. Then quick thinking and faster reflexes had gotten him out of the choke hold, but the reason he was still drawing breath was because Don Emilio didn't want him dead, yet. Not that the temporary dispensation had stopped the Brethren from shooting up the cabin.

Dread had him in a viselike grip until he burst through the tree line onto the Nelsons' property.

Dr. Evander Nelson, a retired veterinarian, stood on his lawn in pajamas and wellies, pointing a rifle at Wendy. She had her hands up in the air and looked like she was trying to reassure Doc that she wasn't the enemy.

Relief at seeing Wendy unharmed hit Jagger so hard that the air whooshed from his lungs. It was all he could do not to go running to her.

With the snap of twigs, Doc swung the rifle in Jagger's direction.

"Hey, Doc! It's me." Jagger's grandmother had been close to the Nelson family, and he maintained a cordial relationship.

Doc pushed his glasses up the bridge of his nose. "Jagger?"

"Yeah. It's me and that's Wendy." Jagger resisted the urge to double over, resting his palms against his thighs, and catch his breath. "You remember her, right?" He walked toward Wendy, taking slow, steady steps.

Doc lowered the rifle. "She told me her name, but she looks so different." He squinted at her. "You can never be too careful."

In his defense, he was pushing eighty. Ten years had passed since he'd met Wendy once and it wasn't as though his eyesight had improved during that time.

"Is all that commotion coming from your place?" Doc asked.

"I'm afraid so."

"That's what I figured. I called the cops."

"Thanks, but we can't stick around. I think it's best if you went inside, took your wife down to the cellar and waited for the trouble to pass."

"You did warn me this might happen someday." Doc made his way to the porch, slowed down by the arthritis in his limbs. "I'll get Gloria and we'll keep our heads down."

"Sorry about the inconvenience, Doc."

The screen door squeaked and slapped shut behind Doc, and then the storm door locked.

"I tried to tell Doc that you needed help, but he didn't remember me," Wendy said, rushing up to him, and he brought her into his arms. "Thank God you're all right." Her fingers tightened around his biceps. "I thought that man might kill you." She cupped his face with both hands and looked him over.

Alaric had come close to hurting him, but Jagger didn't want to find out why Don Emilio had spared him. They had dodged a bullet at the cabin, literally and figuratively.

"I'm all right. You did good, finding the zip line and taking it here."

"I was going to go back for you, but Doc held me up."

A good thing he had, too. If she had returned to the cabin to try to help him, it only would've put her back in the Brethren's crosshairs. "Next time, don't ever think about going back for me."

"To hell with that. We get through this together or not

at all." She pressed her forehead to his chest. "But let's hope there's not a next time."

He loved her fire and determination though sometimes that stubborn streak of hers drove him crazy. "We need to keep moving."

Jagger guided her to the detached garage that had tiny string lights hung around the edge of the roof. After entering the code on the combination padlock, he opened the roll-up door. Inside was the vintage car his father had left him. A 1970s Mercedes-Benz SL-Class Roadster.

"What's your car doing here?"

"It's a long story."

They hurried into the garage and climbed into the two-seat pagoda coupe. He pulled down the visor and the keys fell into his palm.

Jagger cranked the engine and the car purred to life. He backed out, sped down the drive to the road and made a beeline for State Route 117.

"Once I had the security system installed at the cabin, I realized I needed another exit. After I came up with the idea for the zip line, I needed someplace safe to attach the other end. The Nelsons are good people. My grandmother trusted them, and they were within range. Doc was happy to help. I've been renting the garage. It kept this old gal out of the elements," he said, patting the walnut dash. "Prevented anyone from sabotaging her. Doc started her up once a week for me."

"*Smart* always was sexy on you." She reached out and put her hand on his cheek, then ran her fingers through his hair, stroking his ear.

He could say the same about *brave* on her. When Alaric had shoved him out the window, his greatest fear hadn't been for himself—it had been for Wendy. Not knowing how many others had gotten inside the cabin, anything could've happened to her while he was powerless to get her to the attic and out of the house.

With the fire and the Brethren attack and the gunfire, it would've been natural for her to freeze, but she'd saved herself. She had the fortitude of a warrior.

"Do you have any idea how they found us?" she asked.

He'd been racking his brain over the same question. "No. I've run through the possibilities, and I keep drawing a blank for the answer." The name on the deed was an LLC his grandmother had established, and no one knew about the house, except for Wendy. Not even Jagger's father.

"What are we supposed to do now that our safe house is toast?"

A sudden heaviness filled Jagger's chest. Their options had shrunk to one.

One he hoped they wouldn't regret. He'd made a deal with the devil three years ago and now he was going to have to call on that devil again.

"Did you get my burner phone by any chance?" he asked.

Wendy squeezed her eyes shut and swore. "I grabbed what I could—ammunition, weapons—but…no. Wait." She opened the backpack and, with a smile, took out her purse. "I still have my cell phone."

Making a call from her phone was dicey, but staying on the move while using the cell before they reached the interstate going either north or south mitigated the risk. Even if the communication was tracked, no one would know which way they were headed or their destination. It was worth the gamble.

She removed the back of her cell, popped the battery in and powered the phone up.

Then he noticed that the SIM card was already in it, but he had taken out both the battery and the SIM card earlier. Told her explicitly not to put them inside the phone.

"Did you call someone back at the cabin?" he asked.

Wendy stiffened, not responding for a heartbeat too long. She glanced at him and her lips parted, but she didn't speak.

"You gave me your word that you wouldn't use the phone." He'd trusted her, believing she understood the possible ramifications. "I told you they can track us through your phone. What were you thinking?"

"It was only for a minute. Less," she breathed. "Not long enough for a trace."

"Thirty seconds. That's how long it takes to trace a call."

"I wasn't on the phone that long." She lowered her head. "He didn't answer. It went straight to voice mail."

"Who didn't answer?" He glanced at her, hiking an eyebrow. "Tripp Langston?"

Her head snapped up. "Are you kidding me?" She pursed her lips and her eyes narrowed. "Tripp is a cold-blooded reptile. He's probably having sex with someone from the gala as we speak instead of wondering what in the hell happened to me."

Jagger tightened his grip on the steering wheel and checked his mirrors. "Then who did you risk our lives to call?"

"My brother. I thought Dutch might be able to help us. This whole situation came out of left field, blindsiding me. At the very least, he could shed a little light on why Emilio Vargas wants me dead."

If anyone had answers, it was Dutch. Vargas was

angry enough at her brother to want Wendy dead. The fact that Dutch's phone went straight to voice mail troubled him.

He didn't let his worry show, not wanting to add to her list of concerns. "I shouldn't have jumped to conclusions, but you should have told me you made a call."

She let out a heavy breath. "I didn't think it was important since his voice mail picked up, which was full by the way. I couldn't even leave a message. He called me a few days ago and told me he was going on an extended vacation with his girlfriend, somewhere remote, and that it would be hard to contact him for a while, but I didn't think he meant impossible. Anyway, I hung up and took the battery out right after."

From the sounds of it, she hadn't been on the phone long. Slim odds that her call had led the Brethren to them, which still left the big question. How did Alaric and the others find them?

Her phone chimed once it was finished powering up.

"I need you to text someone." He gave her the number. "Write this. *It's JC. Need to meet ASAP.*"

She typed the message and hit Send. As she went to shut off the phone, a chirp from a replying text came through. "That was quick."

"What does it say?"

Wendy looked at the screen: "Usual spot. One hour."

"Respond with *okay*, and shut off the phone."

She did and then removed the battery and SIM card. "Who did we contact?"

"The FBI. Special Agent Eddie Morton."

Shock washed across her face and her eyes brightened. "You have connections with the FBI?"

"Unfortunately."

"Why didn't you call this special agent for help sooner?"

"Because his help always comes at a high price." Agreeing to work for Morton, signing away his soul, had been a mistake. "He's more trouble than he's worth."

"How long have you been working with the FBI?" she asked.

"Three years."

The surprise in her eyes morphed into understanding. "The FBI got you out of prison early."

He nodded. "Two days after I was sent to Sing Sing, Special Agent Morton came to see me."

"Why?"

There were things about his past and his family that he hadn't wanted Wendy to know—footnotes that he never thought would have a bearing on his life. He couldn't have been more wrong.

"My father used to be Emilio Vargas's lawyer. I grew up around the cartel."

Wendy gave a soft gasp of surprise. "What?"

"My dad never wanted me to do business with them, become one of them. He also didn't want me to be naive about that world. The lure of it. The dangers. Some parents protect their kids by keeping them in the dark, insulating them in a bubble. Not my dad. He had the opposite philosophy."

"You know Emilio Vargas?"

"I do." Very well in fact. "And his son, Miguel."

"Please don't tell me that the man who is trying to kill me is your godfather or that you call him uncle."

"I don't have a godfather." But if he did, it would've been Emilio. "And no, I've never called him *uncle*."

Wendy shook her head slowly. "We shared everything

with each other. Or I thought we had. Apparently not. Why didn't you ever tell me this?"

"I possessed none of the things your mother wanted for you. No college degree, no future in business… I was a blue-collar worker."

"My mom didn't care that you were a mechanic. She thought our relationship was too intense and moving too fast, especially after we started living together. She feared I'd get pregnant, drop out of school and we'd get married. My mom didn't understand that we were both being careful, using protection, that we had a five-year plan. She couldn't see what we shared. How real it was."

The words pulled him back to when he'd been the happiest. It had been an intense year and a half. An all-consuming relationship. Wendy had been it for him. The one. "Let's not forget that it was also a problem for her that I was a lot older."

"Only four years."

"In your mom's defense, you were seventeen, and the age gap probably felt as wide as the Grand Canyon. I understood those concerns, respected them, and that's why I took things slow in the beginning." Slower than he'd thought himself capable of, considering he'd wanted her the first day they met and she'd never been shy about her desire for him. "The one thing I had going for me was that I'd been a Ranger." Not that it had mattered much to her mother, but it had made every difference with Dutch, who had been Delta Force, and with that brought a mutual respect. "My past association with the cartel would have added legitimate fuel to the fire."

Her shoulders fell. "I get why you didn't want my mom to know," she said, putting her hand on his leg.

That's all it took to have his body soften in response, aching to draw her closer.

"Why not tell me?" she asked. "It was a part of who you were…who you are."

"After I joined the army, I put a lot of distance between me and the cartel. It was behind me, and I didn't want you to have to lie to your family about me. To feel you had to hide something from them."

"Always protecting me." She gave his knee a squeeze of understanding and rubbed his thigh.

He soaked in the affection he'd missed for a decade, no matter how small the gesture. The longing had been an itch deep in his soul that never went away.

"What does the FBI want with you?" she asked.

"The FBI tried to get my father to flip on Emilio for many years, and every time they failed. When I got convicted, I guess I came up on their radar. Agent Morton approached me. Asked me to get inside the cartel and help them bring down the Brethren. They figured if they got enough of the hit men, they could get them to turn on Miguel and Emilio. Bring down the entire cartel on that angle instead of drugs, money laundering or racketeering. In exchange, the FBI offered to commute my sentence."

"So you agreed."

"Not at first. My father never turned on Emilio. I was raised to value loyalty, even to the cartel, but violent things started to happen to me in jail. Other groups began targeting me for no apparent reason. Looking back on it, I think Morton instigated it somehow."

"Why would he endanger you like that?"

"It forced to me to go to the cartel for protection. Then my cell was changed, and they put me in with Sixty."

"You think Morton was behind that, too?"

Every instinctive bone in his body said Morton was the man behind the curtain pulling the strings. "Yeah, I do, not that I have any proof. I don't trust him. He's calculating, strategic. The kind of man who likes to play the long game."

"You were in jail for years, why didn't you take his deal sooner?"

"He finally offered me what I really wanted. To have my conviction expunged." Remove his criminal record entirely and make it look as if it never happened. "Give me a fresh start as a free man, a decorated veteran, instead of a convicted felon. Give me a real stab at a second chance with you. I could call you, knock on your door, without tainting your life and destroying your business."

That was the goal. Not an easy one. Jagger still needed to provide enough evidence to bring down the Brethren to have his record erased.

"Oh, Jagger. You've been so busy protecting me, trying to make sure nothing hurts me. I wish you would've given me the chance to do the same for you," she whispered, her hand moving from his leg to stroke the back of his neck. "If you had called me, knocked on my door, and been honest, the way you were at the cabin, our second chance would've started right then and there. I don't need you to protect my career. I've done a pretty good job of taking care of myself since you've been gone."

"I didn't want you to sacrifice anything."

"You sacrificed seven years for me. I could stomach a little a bad press for you." A sad smile tugged at her mouth. "I know you don't trust Special Agent Morton, but he has to help us. Doesn't he?"

"I'm not holding my breath, but we're out of options."

"So… What's the usual spot where you meet him, and what's our plan?"

Chapter Thirteen

After parking the car in an outrageously expensive garage—one reason Wendy had never owned a car while living in the city—they swung by a drugstore in Midtown Manhattan.

Mr. Always Prepared picked up a couple of essentials while she found temporary hair dye spray that transformed her locks from caramel blond to raven black. Still, as they hurried down Lexington Avenue, they both purchased ball caps from a street vendor.

There was a light chill in the air. She was glad for the windbreakers they wore. The air smelled damp and clean, and the pavement was wet from the rain that had fallen earlier.

He took her hand in his, the way he used to when they were a couple strolling the street, their fingers interlaced.

The action flipped a switch inside her that she didn't want to turn off. Every day they'd spent apart, a piece of her heart had been missing, and now that he was back she didn't want to let go of him. Not ever again.

Inside Grand Central Station in the large vestibule, Jagger pointed out the seven different pedestrian exits on a map.

"Why do the two of you meet here?"

"It's open twenty-one hours a day and it's the largest train station in the world."

To call it massive, with its grandiose structure, soaring high ceilings and acres of smooth pink marble floors, was an understatement. She'd been inside before but had never really appreciated the scale until now.

"Hundreds of thousands of people pass through here every day," he said. "Makes it easy to blend in and go unnoticed any time of day or night." Even now, the station was bustling with foot traffic. He grabbed a train schedule and handed it to her. "You know what to do?"

Her job was to stay focused on the time and the departure schedule of the trains, giving him a chance to concentrate on the discussion with Special Agent Morton. In the event the Brethren showed up, Jagger was relying on her to get them out of Grand Central in the most expedient way possible.

"I've got it." Wendy's stomach grumbled.

Jagger looked down at her and grinned. "I suppose I'll need to feed you."

"I can't be the only one starving."

He glanced around, checking their surroundings. "You're not. After the meeting with Morton, we'll worry about food."

They walked through the main concourse, past corridors and nooks, and into the Graybar Passage. The arched corridor was lined with shops and kiosks that were open late. Jagger led her into the Central Market, and they turned into a café.

"That's him there." Jagger gestured to a man sitting a table, sipping a beverage in a disposable cup with a lid.

Special Agent Morton was in his early fifties. He had a soft middle section and a feathering of gray in his beard.

"Normally," Jagger said, "I sit at the table next to his and we pretend to read while we chat. I'd rather keep moving, but he's not going to like the change in protocol."

Considering the Brethren had tracked them down at the cabin and they were still none the wiser as to how, she was inclined to agree that they couldn't afford to make themselves sitting ducks.

"Wait here."

She hung back near the entrance, looking at a poster of the café's seasonal specials.

In the coffee shop, Jagger waltzed up to Morton and motioned for the middle-aged man to get up.

Morton's face tightened with suspicion as he looked around. It took a bit more prodding from Jagger, but finally the agent grabbed his cup and started walking.

"This better be good, JC," Morton said as the two passed her in the corridor. "I got out of bed for this."

"It's about the cartel."

Wendy walked behind them, staying within earshot.

"Do you have what I need?" Morton asked. "Evidence to bring down the Brethren?"

"No."

Morton clucked his tongue. "This is a waste of my time."

"What I do have is her." Jagger beckoned to her and she came up alongside him.

Special Agent Morton peered over at her, studying her face for a moment. "Wendy Haas, as I live and breathe. I almost didn't recognize you from the pictures in his file. I'll admit, I'm surprised." He sipped on his drink. "Now, please explain how your ex-girlfriend's presence helps my case against the cartel."

"Emilio Vargas put a hit out on me," she said. "I'm only alive thanks to Jagger."

Morton nodded as if taking it in, with no hint of emotion on his face other than a look of boredom. "Elaborate."

"A kill order was issued on her tonight," Jagger said as they entered the main concourse. "A blood debt. The entire Brethren is after her." He scanned the area as they walked through the crowd of commuters.

"After *us*," she clarified. They both needed protection.

"They know I'm helping her," Jagger said. "Which means they're after me as well."

Wendy noted the time on the clock adorning the terminal's information booth and checked the subway schedule. The 4, 5, 6 and 7 trains were viable options with three different access points to the subway platform on this level.

"My interest is piqued. Did Vargas issue the order personally?" Morton asked.

"No." Jagger shook his head. "He's in prison."

"*Was* in prison," Special Agent Morton said.

Wendy glanced between the two men. "What do you mean?"

"He escaped and is in the wind," Morton said. "It's all over the news, and of course his son, Miguel, is conveniently out of the country, so we can't question him."

Jagger looked around the concourse as they strolled the periphery. "Yeah, well, we've been too busy running for our lives to watch television."

"You could always listen to NPR," Morton said, casually. "No excuse for not staying informed."

Wendy's patience frayed. "Are you going to help us?"

she asked, painfully aware they'd been in one place far too long.

"Help with what exactly?" Morton sounded dismissive.

Wendy glared at him. "Help us stay alive. Put us in protective custody."

Morton chuckled. "If I did, how does that help me get a conviction that'll bring down Miguel Vargas, the Brethren or the cartel? All I'm hearing is what you think I can do for you and not what you can do for me or rather your country."

"I served my country." Jagger stopped in front of a news and gift kiosk and faced Morton. "Gave four honorable years."

"Thanks for your service, JC. I mean that from the bottom of my heart."

"Help her." Jagger pointed at Wendy. "Put her somewhere safe and I'll get the evidence you need."

"No, Jagger." She clutched his arm. "We stay together. He has to protect us both."

Morton tossed his cup into a trash bin. "That's where you're wrong."

"You have a civic duty, an obligation, to keep us safe." Didn't he?

"Not my jurisdiction." Morton had the audacity to yawn. "Go to the police. It's their job to keep you safe."

"You know as well as I do that if I take her to the cops," Jagger said, "the Brethren will kill her in less than twenty-four hours."

"You're absolutely right. I agree." Morton crossed his arms as if preparing to go on the defense. "If you bring me your cartel buddies after they kill her, I can put pressure on them to flip on Los Chacales."

Wendy had heard horror stories about FBI negotiations, agents playing hardball in a game of the end justifies the means, but this was unreal. "You can't be serious. Is this some kind of sick joke?"

"I never joke, Ms. Haas. My wife says I don't have a sense of humor."

She stepped forward, looking him in the eye. "How can you sit back and let them kill me?"

"The same way I stood by and let your boyfriend here kill people in the name of the Brethren to cement his cover story," Morton said.

The statement hit her like a bucket of ice water. "You're lying." Wendy rocked back on her heels as her gaze flew to Jagger's. "You didn't. You wouldn't." That was too ugly, going too far.

"I can explain." Jagger gripped her shoulders. "It's not how it sounds."

Oh, God. It was true.

"Think of yourself as a sacrificial lamb, Ms. Haas," Morton said matter-of-factly. "Your death would light a fire under him to give me the evidence I need to finally stop the Brethren and save countless other lives. I know that may sound callous."

"May?" She breathed through the bitter taste in her mouth.

"Los Chacales cartel has survived, no, has thrived and grown and is now one of the top threats to national security. It is a massive thorn in the FBI's side as well as the president's. We have an entire task force dedicated to nothing but the annihilation of Los Chacales cartel. If I have to be callous to get results, then so be it."

Jagger's head turned toward the MetLife Building entrance.

As Wendy followed his gaze, a tingle of apprehension skittered across her skin.

Two men dressed in black came through the doors. One was holding a phone or a device and was staring at the screen. Then he looked up and pointed in their direction.

"Our time's up. Start walking toward the trains," Jagger said to her. "I'll be right behind you."

Although she didn't want to leave him, she followed his instruction.

"Thanks for nothing, Morton," Jagger said behind her and she missed the rest of his words as she turned down the Forty-second Street passage. Jagger caught up to her. "Which train?"

"The 6 is our best bet, going uptown, but we have less than two minutes. We'll miss it unless we run."

"Not yet. Once we make the turn for the platforms, I'll tell you when." He glanced over his shoulder as he tightened the straps on the backpack that he carried. "They're closing in."

Two more men stormed in through the Forty-second Street entrance.

They both lowered their heads and rounded the corner into the passageway that led to the trains.

Jagger stuck his hand into his pocket and took out the bottle of baby oil he'd purchased in the drugstore. "Now. Run," he said, discreetly squirting the mineral oil in a swath behind them.

Wendy took off down the passageway, sprinting toward the platform. She sneaked a glance back before she hit the escalator and lost sight of him.

Jagger bolted after her, gesturing for her to keep going with one hand, while he emptied the full bottle.

The four men charged down the corridor, shoving people out of their way. Other commuters veered to the sides. As soon as the men hit the slick patch of marble, going at an all-out sprint, there was no time for them to adjust and keep their balance. They slipped and gravity did the rest, taking them down.

The slippery surface wouldn't stop them, but it slowed them down. A few precious seconds. Perhaps time enough for them to get away.

She reached the escalator and ran down the moving steel stairs. A train was pulling into the station.

A distinctive sound echoed behind her and screams followed, but she didn't stop. It was gunfire. Suppressed but loud enough to draw the Transit cops.

The doors of the train opened, and one stream of pedestrians poured out as another flowed into the subway cars.

At the platform, she looked back. Jagger was making his way down the escalator, cutting around those standing still on the moving staircase.

She hurried onto the train and waited. Her chest tightened, her heart pounding in her throat.

Come on, Jagger. Hurry. Seconds ticked through her. Nerves rolled her stomach, making her feel that she might be sick.

A chime sounded and the automated voice announced, "Stand clear of the closing doors please."

No, no, no. She wasn't going to leave Jagger behind. No matter the consequences.

Two more shots echoed, sending a chill up her spine. The doors started to close, and she thrust her arm between them, triggering the train's conductor to pop them open again.

Another chime and repeat of the automated message.

Jagger hopped off the escalator, dashed across the platform and darted onto the train.

The doors slid closed behind him and the train lurched, rolling forward, inching out of the station.

The four men spilled off the escalator and slipped across the platform. One fired at them, but the bullet pinged into metal as the train entered the dark tunnel.

Trembling, Wendy leaned against Jagger and pressed her cheek to his chest. He took her into his arms and held her as if he understood that she needed a minute for the world to stop spinning. His heart beat strong and fast, the steady rhythm a comfort against her cheek. His hands were warm on her head and her lower back, and his body heat did the trick of chasing the cold from her skin until she could breathe again.

"Wendy, I need to explain," he said, his voice a low rumble in her ear, "about the things Morton told you."

She stiffened at remembering. Jagger had willingly killed people for the Brethren.

His arms tightened around her as if he feared losing her, and suddenly nothing was certain. "I did what he said. But I chose the assignments I accepted with Morton. To make sure that the people the Brethren sent me after were bad. Criminals and scumbags the world wouldn't miss. It was the only way I could be part of the organization without raising suspicion." He stroked his hands down her hair, rubbed his cheek against her temple. "You know me. Please, honey. You *know* me."

He repeated the words, a mantra, over and over. A sob rocked through her, but she reined it in. The truth was, she did know him. His heart. His soul. He was principled and kind.

Jagger would never hurt an innocent person, much less take their life. Everything he'd done, from going to prison to getting tangled up with the Brethren had been for her. To find his way back to her.

With that came guilt, an inescapable sense of responsibility, because deep down there wasn't anything she wouldn't do to have a second chance with Jagger.

To get closer to him, she tucked her feet between his boots, pressed into him and looked up, meeting his gaze. "I love you. I've never stopped. Never will."

Relief was heavy in his eyes. Jagger dropped a kiss on her forehead.

The train emerged from the tunnel, pulling into the next station.

"We can't keep running like this," she said, low.

"We have to figure out how they're tracking us. I know someone who might have the answer."

The train stopped and the doors opened.

They hustled onto the platform and ran up the steps.

"If they're on motorcycles, they could be here any minute," Jagger said.

They made their way through the turnstile and raced outside into the fresh air. Jagger waved down a taxi. They climbed in and he gave the driver an address.

"Who are we going to see?" she asked.

"Pilar Zahiri."

Wendy's stomach knotted. The name was unusual and familiar. Very familiar. "Your ex-girlfriend?"

Jagger sighed. "She was never my girlfriend."

"You slept with her. She was your first."

Another sigh. "We were childhood friends. It was a one-time thing. A lifetime ago."

"She's in the cartel?"

He nodded.

"Have you seen her since you were released?"

Jagger lowered his head and the knot in her belly clenched harder. "Not in the way you think."

"How do you know what I'm thinking?"

"It doesn't matter. Whatever you're thinking, it wasn't like that. Not as old friends. Not as acquaintances."

"Maybe it was for another one-time thing. I'm sure you've been with someone in the last three years and there's nothing wrong with that." Even if it hurt that it hadn't been with her. "Just don't hide it from me."

"I was with someone. A one-night stand, but it wasn't with her. Pilar is in the Brethren, or rather she used to be. Now, she's with Miguel."

"Vargas?" she whispered.

"Yep. She's now his…lady. I've seen her because of my dealings with Miguel."

"Why on earth do you think she'd help us?"

"Not us. Me. We have history and I know she's not happy. Correction, she is a woman with an ax to grind, hiding it behind a smile. She hooked up with Miguel as a power play, hoping that he'd grant her his favor and move her up the ranks in the Brethren. It backfired. He pulled her altogether, claiming he loved her too much to have her soiling her hands or putting herself in harm's way."

"Isn't that a good thing? That he loves her enough to want to keep her safe?"

"Miguel loves her about as much as he loves his Ferrari. Actually, he might love his car more. She wanted power, and he put a leash on her ambition instead. It's turned into this sick game of control between them, and for her there's no winning. No way out. She's stuck. It's a shame, too, because she's smart as a whip, speaks five languages, strong, ruthless when necessary, keeps her ear to ground on everything. She'd make a good partner for him, but he's not willing to let her rule *with* him. Then again, maybe he's worried that if he gave her the power she wants, she'd slit his throat in the night and take the entire kingdom."

They were going to Lady Macbeth on steroids for assistance. "Do you really think that she's bitter enough to betray Miguel by helping you?"

He shrugged. "I hope so. You know what they say. Hell hath no fury like a woman scorned."

Chapter Fourteen

"Are you sure she'll be here?" Wendy asked, feeling self-conscious as they walked through the Hotel Duchand's swanky bar wearing jeans and windbreakers.

The idea of approaching Pilar hadn't grown on her. There were too many ways this could go wrong, but she didn't have a better alternative.

"She lives here on the top floor with Miguel in a lavish penthouse suite. When he's not in town, she has a tendency to drink at the bar."

Wendy wasn't going to dive back into the jealousy pool by asking how he knew that detail.

"I see her. She's with her driver." Jagger let go of Wendy's hand and walked up to a striking woman sitting at the bar, talking to a man in a suit. She wore a white one-shoulder leather dress that hugged her slender figure like a second skin and sky-high heels. She had long, toned legs that were evidence of serious commitment to the gym and shiny dark hair that fell to her waist.

Wendy trailed behind Jagger, giving him a little space while still staying close enough to hear the conversation.

"Pilar."

The woman turned, giving Wendy a chance to see how drop-dead gorgeous she was. Pilar slunk off the bar stool with the grace of a viper, hugged him and kissed both his cheeks.

A hot knife of jealousy stabbed Wendy at the show of genuine affection between them.

"Jagger? What are you doing here?" In her heels she was as tall as Jagger, and she looked like a damn swimsuit model. Not a former hit woman.

"I need to talk to you. It's urgent. Can we do it in your car? Now?"

The look of confusion crossing her face was fleeting. "Of course. Ronaldo," she said, motioning to her driver.

The man got up and led the way out of the bar.

As Pilar snaked her arm around Jagger's, she gave Wendy a sidelong glance. "Is she with you?"

He held out his hand to Wendy and brought her in close on the opposite side of him. "She is."

A smirk curved Pilar's glossy red lips. One of her perfectly plucked eyebrows lifted, and her nose crinkled in an expression of curiosity.

"Time is of the essence," Jagger said.

Pilar straightened, letting him go, and strutted off in front of them.

"Still sure about this?" Wendy whispered. "She looked a little possessive of you."

"It's nothing. She respects me, cares for me, but like a sister. I promise." He wrapped an arm around her shoulder and squeezed—a bit of reassurance, also maybe a warning. They were working against the clock and desperately needed answers.

They piled into her car, which was parked out front. If you could call a fully loaded four-hundred-thousand-dollar extended Maybach that seated four in the back simply a car.

"Can you ask him to drive around? Keep us moving?" Jagger asked, seated beside Wendy and across from Pilar.

"Certainly." Pilar relayed Jagger's instructions and then rolled up the tinted privacy partition.

Jagger waited until the car was in motion on the road. "Where's Miguel?"

"Overseas. Doing business. I suspect you already know that if you came looking for me at the bar."

"Why didn't you go with him?" Jagger asked.

She flashed a smile and let out a throaty chuckle. "Isn't it pathetic enough that I'm arm candy in the States. Must I be reduced to a useless sexual trophy in Europe as well? Besides, it gives Miguel an opportunity to do his on-the-side gallivanting without rubbing my face in it."

A scorned woman, indeed. Pilar might help them after all.

Jagger leaned forward. "Do you know about the recent kill order?"

"I'm aware that something big came down the pike."

"Do you know why Emilio claims a blood debt?"

Pilar crossed her legs. "Why does it matter?"

"This is the target. Wendy Haas. The Brethren have been tracking us. Everywhere we go, they turn up."

"So, you come to me!" Outrage washed across her face. "Sorry, I can't help you."

"Pilar, you're the only person who can help me. Please, wouldn't you love to get back at Miguel? Feel like you have the power to do something. Exercise that God-given free will unless you're happy being a pretty puppet for the rest of your life."

"Don't try to get in my head, *guerrero guapo*." She called him *handsome warrior* as she pointed a finger at him. Her long, manicured nail looked like a talon.

"I just need you to answer a couple of questions. I'm begging."

"That's a first. You never beg." She let out a heavy breath and pulled a flask from her purse. "Make it fast."

"Why does Emilio want her dead?"

"Quite a few radioactive bombshells have dropped in the Vargas household recently." She unscrewed the top on the flask and took a long pull. "Emilio doesn't care about you," Pilar said, looking at Wendy. "He's angry at your brother. More like spitting mad really."

"This is about Dutch," Jagger said. "I knew it."

"But why?" Wendy asked. "What did my brother do?"

"He went undercover for the US Marshals to get close to Emilio."

Wendy shook her head. "That doesn't sound like him. He works in fugitive recovery."

"Listen, sweetheart, we don't have time for all the interruptions as you wrap your brain around what I'm saying."

Wendy stiffened, and Jagger patted her leg and cast her a pleading look to let it go.

Pilar caught the look and his hand on Wendy's leg, and there was a flash of something heated in her eyes.

"As I was saying," Pilar continued, "your brother went undercover and seduced Isabel."

That was the name of Dutch's new girlfriend, the one he mentioned taking an extended vacation with. Was this story true?

"Isabel? Emilio's niece?" Jagger asked.

"Turns out, Isabel is his daughter. And that marshal, your brother, made her believe she was in love and convinced her to turn against Emilio."

"What?" The alarm in Jagger's voice told Wendy the situation was worse than he'd anticipated.

"Miguel is hot under the collar about not knowing Isabel was his half sister all this time and about some old affair being the reason his mother left. *Boo-hoo*, I say, but Miguel refused to help break Emilio out of prison. That's the real reason Miguel is overseas. Hiding from daddy and having a tantrum." Pilar rolled her eyes. "So, I graciously stepped up to facilitate arrangements for Emilio outside of El Paso."

"But why does he want me dead?" Wendy asked.

"Emilio feels that since Dutch stole his daughter and stirred the proverbial pot, he's going to punish him by killing you." Pilar swung a talon in Wendy's direction. "It's an old-school underworld way of handling a grievance. An eye for an eye. In my opinion, it's overkill. No pun intended. But no one gives two flying figs what I think."

Wendy folded her hands, resisting the urge to scrub her sweaty palms on her thighs. "How do we get Emilio Vargas to rescind the kill order?"

Pilar turned her dazzling fake smile on Wendy. "You're cute. Your naivete works for you, like a beautiful accessory." Her gaze bounced to Jagger. "I can see the appeal," she said, and then looked back at Wendy. "The kill order will only go away if the Brethren completes their task, or…you two kill Emilio first."

A fresh wave of nausea rolled over her. Both options were unfathomable.

"How are they tracking us?" Jagger asked.

"Why are you helping her?" Pilar turned the flask up to her lips again. "Disloyalty isn't a good look on you."

Jagger sat back. "It's none of your business."

"You made it my business, *guapo*, the second you came to me. Now, either you tell me, or I have Ronaldo stop, let the two of you out, and you'll never know how they keep finding you." She glanced between them. "It's rude to waste my time. Not to mention dangerous for all parties."

"My murder charge," he said, taking Wendy's hand. "She's the woman I was involved with at the time."

Pilar's dark eyes lit up like hundred-watt bulbs. "This is the love of your life?" She licked her red lips in a predatory way that made Wendy's skin crawl. "My, the plot thickens."

"How do they keep finding us?" Wendy asked, wanting to get the hell out of the car and as far away from Pilar as possible.

"Remember the rumors about repo?" Pilar took another swig.

"Yeah." Jagger nodded. "That if anyone in the Brethren stepped out of line, they would be repo'd."

"As in repossessed, like property?" Wendy asked.

"Exactly. Turns out, it's not a rumor. It's real. Before they tattooed us, when they gave us our brand," Pilar said, tapping a spot on her chest, over her heart, which was covered by her dress, "it was to hide the fact that they were implanting a GPS tracker in us. That's only one of the more horrifying things I've learned as Miguel's *woman*. They don't want the Brethren knowing about the fail-safe, but you going rogue has forced them to tip their hand."

"I've got to cut it out." Jagger rubbed his chest.

"Good luck with that. It's below the hypodermis layer of skin and could've migrated anywhere in your chest at this point. There's only way to circumvent it."

"Care to share?" he asked.

Pilar put the flask to her lips, and down the hatch went another sip. "You have to die."

"What?" Wendy asked, horrified. "No. There has to be another way."

"It sucks. I know. Imagine how I feel. Everywhere I go Miguel knows it. He's probably tracking me this very moment." Pilar stilled, her gaze roaming as if she was thinking about something. Then she swore in Spanish and French. "If he's tracking both of us, then he knows we're together." Pilar had the driver pull over. "If Miguel questions me about it, I'll say you came to me for help, but I tried to kill you and you got away. Understand."

"How do I disable the tracker?"

"Four hundred volts of electricity should do the trick, but make sure you stay on the move." Pilar kissed Jagger on the lips and opened the car door. *"Buena suerte, hermano."*

Chapter Fifteen

Jagger hailed the first taxi he spotted. "Central Park," he said to the cabbie, and the taxi cut into traffic.

"Why the park?" Wendy asked.

"I only told him that to get us going until we know our next step."

"You have lipstick on your face." Wendy frowned and wiped it from his lip with her thumb. "Do you trust the information Pilar gave us?"

Going to see Pilar had been a gamble, but worth the risk. "She had no reason to lie. It would've been easier for her not to speak to us at all and she told us more than she needed to."

In fact, he now saw a way to save Wendy. What had once been impossible had become feasible, but first he had to deal with the GPS tracker.

"She did spill her guts, but I can't believe Dutch would seduce someone for his job."

"I agree, it doesn't sound like him. Maybe he really fell for Isabel. Sounds as if her feelings for him might be genuine if she betrayed Emilio."

The idea that Isabel was Emilio's daughter still made Jagger's stomach turn. The infidelity, the magnitude of the betrayal and the years of lying boggled his mind. He understood why Miguel was upset, and rightfully so.

Jagger had been in the army when Luis, Emilio's brother had been killed. He'd always assumed it had happened in a turf war with a rival cartel. What if it had been something altogether different, perhaps infighting between the brothers?

This would also explain Emilio's desire for a blood debt. No one messed with his family. Especially not his son or his daughter. That was probably a secret Emilio had planned to carry to his grave.

A dangerous, powerful man with a vendetta was on the warpath, making life-ending decisions based on hot-blooded emotions.

"It can't be easy to lose the ones you love. First, his daughter and, based on what Pilar said, his son is turning his back on him," Wendy said, showing the depth of her compassion, even for a man who had put a hit out on her.

"Maybe the discord between Emilio and Miguel could be used to our benefit somehow. If Miguel refused to help break his father out of jail, that's big." An indication of a major rift between them.

This was such a mess.

Wendy rubbed her forehead on a sigh. "That brings me back to Pilar. Why did she tell you so much?"

"She still has a soft spot for me. I would've helped her if the situation had been reversed."

"I don't trust her."

"You don't like her. That's not the same thing."

She straightened with a jerk. "You're right. I don't like her, any more than she likes me. I also don't trust her."

Green was not Wendy's color. "You can't seriously

be jealous." Though this fiery, territorial interest in him was something he was glad she hadn't lost.

"Cut me some slack. It's hard not to be jealous of Pilar Zahiri."

The sentiment wasn't a foreign one to him. He'd always wanted Wendy to be happy, to move on with her life, live it to the fullest. But when he had seen her with Tripp Langston—the stockbroker's arm draped around her waist, holding her close as they posed for pictures— tightness had threaded Jagger's chest, as well as a ringing in his ears worse than fingernails on chalkboard.

"Sure, Pilar is beautiful," he said, "in the same way a sword is. A work of art capable of slitting your throat. Miguel probably sleeps with one eye open. There's no competition between the two of you, believe me. You're warm, kind, and you love with your whole heart. That takes a type of courage someone like Pilar will never understand."

Wendy's love, so fearless and undeniable, had been the air he breathed, and for the past decade, he'd been suffocating without her. She was still everything he wanted. Needed. His ideal partner. Once you had experienced *ideal* it was damn near impossible to settle for anything less.

Her fingers found his, and they did a little intimate dance as he enjoyed the feel of her beside him.

"I'm sorry," Wendy said. "It was the first time I've been face-to-face with someone you've slept with and still care about. Does Miguel know that you and Pilar were once together?"

"No. It wouldn't do either one of us any good if he knew. Besides, it's ancient history. Our feelings for each other are fraternal, not romantic."

She blew out a breath. "My personal feelings aside, she strikes me as the type of person who would only help if she was getting something in return. Is thumbing her nose at Miguel with her little act of defiance enough for her?"

"Pilar put herself on the line for us when she didn't have to."

Wendy tipped her head back and looked up at him. "Not us. You, *guerrero guapo*."

Jagger wrapped his arm around her shoulder. "Thanks to her we know how they're tracking us." Without that tidbit, they'd still be running around the city clueless while being stalked, and then it would've only been a matter of time. Pilar might have saved their lives.

"But what are we supposed to do about it? Use a Taser on you, or a stun gun?"

"I don't think that has enough juice. The voltage is high enough on one of those, but the amperage is way too low. We need to think in terms of electrocution to short circuit the GPS tracker. Maybe we use a car battery and jumper cables."

Wendy's face twisted in horror that he too felt but didn't show. "Are you insane? What if something goes wrong? What if you actually die and I..." Her voice trailed off.

"You what?"

"I know where we need to go." Wendy leaned forward and tapped on the plexiglass partition. "Excuse me," she said to the driver. "Change of plans. Instead of Central Park, we need you to drop us somewhere else." She gave him an address Jagger didn't recognize.

"You want the hospital?" the cabbie asked.

"Yes."

"There's a closer one," the driver said.

"No, take us to the address I gave you."

"It's your money, lady." He put on the turn signal and changed lanes.

Jagger sat up. "We can't go to a hospital, remember."

"We can't be put in the system, but the hospital is exactly what we need. I know an ER doctor. He was a client."

"What's his name?"

"Fitz. Fitzgerald Gilmore."

That was a mouthful.

The doctor was a client she had gone out with. He'd been in her dating lineup after the lawyer. Voicing that knowledge would only support the idea that Jagger was a stalker, but Wendy didn't want him to hide things.

"I know you had a fling. I don't care. Ancient history, right? And it'd be great if you didn't care how I know."

Wendy glared at him and shook her head. "I don't care that you kept tabs on me," she said, and he silently thanked her for not using the creepy *S* word. "I care that you didn't contact me. Three wasted years when we could've been fighting for our second chance."

She made it sound so simple when it was anything but. Still wasn't as long as he was a convicted felon. The emotional baggage between them was heavy and real. Every time they dug below the surface of it, they found bruises—on their hearts, on their egos.

For now, he'd focus on the doctor.

If memory served, Fitz had been sued for malpractice and beaten it with a settlement. His reputation had taken a major hit, according to the papers, and it looked as if the hospital was going to let him go. In swooped Wendy, a PR superhero, and transformed Dr. Code Blue into The Doctor Who'll Pull You Through.

Maybe Dr. Code Blue was who they needed after all.

"My phone." She held out her hand. "It'll be faster if I call him and give him a heads-up."

He fished her phone and battery out of the backpack on the floor between his legs and gave it to her.

She powered it up and made the call. "Hi, Fitz, it's Wendy. This isn't a social call. If you could just hear me out before you say anything. I'm with a friend, someone very important to me. We're in danger, but you can help. I need you use a defibrillator on him and make sure that he doesn't die."

Her gaze dropped as she listened.

"I can't explain why," she said, her words low and fast, "but if you don't do this, then my friend and I are both as good as dead. You'll be responsible for two deaths for certain. If you don't help and I do survive, a certain story about you and black-market organ transplants might get leaked to the media. Before you know it you'll find yourself neck deep in bad press, and that'll be the end of your career."

That nugget hadn't been in the papers. The doctor had a dirty past and a lot to lose.

"Please, don't think of it as blackmail. I'm giving you an incentive to help me. I would never do this unless I had no choice. Fitz, please, I need you." She was quiet for a moment. "Thank you. There's one other thing. You'll need to do it in an ambulance because we have to keep moving. Don't ask, it'll only raise more questions." A long pause. "Okay, we'll see you in a few minutes."

THE TAXI DRIVER stopped by the Emergency Room entrance. Jagger peeled off two tens and paid the cabbie, letting him keep the change.

"Wendy!" A man in blue scrubs waved them over to a different part of the parking lot, where three ambulances were parked.

They ran to the back of the ambulance that had the engine running and an EMT sitting behind the wheel.

Fitz greeted them and helped Wendy up into the back. He was average height, fit, designer stubble, intense eyes, curly brown hair. Radiated calm control. A good trait for an ER doctor. He looked younger in person than he had in the paper. Maybe late twenties, early thirties.

It occurred to Jagger that Wendy catered to a specific demographic. All her clients were millennials.

"You're going to have to pay the tech." Fitz gestured to the driver as they pulled out of the hospital parking lot.

"Will a hundred do it?" Jagger asked.

Fitz's mouth flattened into a thin line. "You better make it two to be on the safe side. I don't need his loose lips damaging my ship."

Jagger dug in his wallet and counted out the money.

Fitz passed the wad of bills to the driver, who stuffed it in his pocket. He directed Jagger to sit on the gurney while he sat on the bench seat beside Wendy and folded his hands. "I understand you can't or won't get into specifics, but in order to help you, it'd be good to know why you need me to hit your bosom buddy with a defibrillator. I take it there's a point and this isn't for recreation."

Wendy stared at Jagger. "It could mean the difference between success and failure if he knew."

"There's a GPS tracker inside me." Jagger took off his windbreaker and pulled up his shirt. "Three years ago, it was inserted here." He pointed to the brand on his chest. "But it could have migrated. We need you to short-circuit it with an electric current. Someone recommended four hundred volts. I honestly don't know if that's enough."

Wendy rested her hand on Fitz's forearm. "We need to be sure that you fry it. There are dangerous people after us. Tracking us as we speak. I also need you to keep him alive."

"Trust me, that's in my best interest as well," Fitz said flatly, not seeming the least bit rattled by the situation, like this was an everyday occurrence.

The doctor's bedside manner inspired confidence.

"The lowest possible voltage is one-forty. It also carries the lowest risk, but if we want to eliminate any doubt about shorting out the device inside you, we should go with five hundred."

Jagger was willing to go as high as necessary, but they had to be sure they fried the GPS tracker. "Five it is."

"Remove your shirt and lie back." Fitz put on latex gloves as Jagger took off his top. "What do we have here?" Fitz asked, inspecting Jagger's patched up wound.

"Gunshot. Superficial. I used superglue on it."

"Looks like you two are having quite the evening. In the future, I don't recommend using superglue. It contains toxins that can be harmful to tissue. Best left in your toolbox and not your medical kit, but if it was the only option to keep you from bleeding out…" Fitz shrugged. "I'll give you a shot of antibiotics so you don't get an infection, just in case."

"Thank you," Wendy said.

Jagger nodded. "Yeah, thanks."

"If you survive this, then you can thank me." Fitz reached over and turned on the defibrillator. "Do you understand that as a healthy individual, you run the risk of cardiac arrest and possible death by proceeding with this?" he asked in an infomercial tone.

The latter was a guarantee if he *didn't* do this. "I understand."

Fitz glanced at Wendy. "Do you understand that if he dies and I can't resuscitate him, the disposal of the body is on you?"

Her face paled and her gaze fixed on Jagger's. The mask slipped. Anguish filled her eyes. It was immense, startling, and seeing it made him ache with regret.

"It won't come to that." In prison, he'd done a lot of reading and come across a myth about how the sun loved the moon so much that he died every night to let her breathe and to put an end to her misery. That's how he thought of his time in jail. He died every day so Wendy could live. Now she needed him to survive. To help her. The universe had messed with him plenty. He had to believe this wouldn't end horrifically. Not for his own sake, but for hers. "I'll get you through this."

She took Jagger's hand and brought it to her lips. Kissed it. Stroked his arm. "If you die on me, I'll never forgive you," she said, her voice shaking, as was her body.

There was so much woven in that statement, simmering beneath the words. He heard it, felt it. All those years ago he thought he was doing the right thing. That if he set her free, it would liberate them both, but all it did was bind them together in an unimaginable way.

She had hurt every day they'd been separated, and it was his fault.

"I can't have that, can I?" He tried to smile but only managed a grin. "I won't leave you alone. I swear it."

"Very touching," Fitz said, deadpan. "Can we get on with it? I'm on call."

"Okay," Jagger said.

"You need to keep your hands off him while I do this," Fitz warned Wendy.

She leaned over and gave Jagger a kiss. It was quick and hard, but he tasted her, got to slide his fingers into hair, absorb the warmth of her touch. For ten damn years, he'd dreamed about lying beside her, holding her, and he wanted it all back. She was the light in the darkness that had saved him from drowning in despair. He wasn't giving up now.

On a gasp, her lips parted and she was about to say something. He put his fingertips over her mouth, stopping her.

"Tell me after," he said. Because they needed to believe that they'd get the chance.

Wendy nodded, her eyes glistening with emotion. "After."

She let his hand go and he stared at her, wanting to hold on to the image of her gorgeous face, no matter what happened.

Fitz adjusted the setting and picked up the defibrillator paddles. "Clear," he said, and pressed them to Jagger's chest.

A searing jolt of agony gripped him, tearing through his body.

Then Wendy and the world slipped away into darkness.

Chapter Sixteen

"Jagger!" Wendy clenched her fists, wanting to shake him until he opened his eyes. When the defibrillator pads had touched him, his whole body had convulsed and popped up inches from the gurney.

"You've got to calm down and be quiet," the EMT said from behind the steering wheel. "Let the doctor work."

Fitz started chest compressions. Jagger's heart had stopped, and he wasn't breathing.

Her anxiety skyrocketed with each passing second that he remained unresponsive.

Fitz checked Jagger's airway, put an oxygen bag mask on him and squeezed. "Hold the bag," he ordered. "Squeeze twice when I tell you."

Wendy scooted forward and held it in her trembling hands as Fitz resumed chest compressions again, much longer than a five count.

Wake up, Jagger. I need you. She prayed for him to open his eyes.

If she lost him a second time, she didn't know if she'd be able to pick up any of the pieces again.

"Squeeze," Fitz hissed at her as he withdrew a syringe from his pocket, tapped it and flicked off that cap. He felt Jagger's left side, pierced his chest wall between his ribs and depressed the plunger, injecting the contents of the syringe.

She swallowed the panic rising in her throat. "What is that?"

"One-milligram epinephrine. Adrenaline. I was hoping we wouldn't need it, but…"

Jagger wasn't responding. They were losing him. The breath in her throat tightened like a fist, refusing to fill her lungs.

Stay with me! Please, God, help him.

Memories crashed over her. Good. Bad. Ugly. Every one of them tied to Jagger. Pent-up grief and loss punched through the surface, shattering something inside her, and tears spilled from her eyes. "Don't leave me," she whispered. "Please, don't leave me again."

Not like this. Cheated out of more time together. It was so unfair.

Fitz began another round of chest compressions, moving faster, pushing with the heel of his palm. He kept pumping to a furious count of thirty as her heart wilted.

Her turn. She squeezed the bag, giving him oxygen.

Holding up a hand for her stop, Fitz put the stethoscope hanging around his neck to Jagger's chest and listened. "We've got a pulse."

Jagger's eyes fluttered and opened. He hauled in a deep breath, glancing around.

Wendy steeled herself to keep from sobbing and clutched his hand. She was too choked up to speak. All she could do was caress his cheek, giving quiet thanks he was back with her.

He looked as weary as she felt. She wished she could give him what little strength she had left.

His gaze settled on her face. "See. I'm not going anywhere. If I make you a promise, I'll keep it." He said it like the vow came straight from his soul.

The words arrowed right through her chest. A whirlwind of emotion stormed inside her, pain from the past, gratitude for this moment, the uncertainty of the future, but one thing burned clearly. "I love you." Her voice trembled. "I'll always love you."

"Good. Because my heart still belongs to you."

He was hers and she was his.

There was no way in hell she was going to lose him again. Not a chance that she would ever walk away or give up on him. Never again.

Fitz sighed. "Speaking of your heart. I'm glad we got it restarted. You'll need to rest, as much as possible for the next twelve hours. That means no more getting shot and drink plenty of fluids." He looked through the upper cabinet for something. "I'll start him on an antibiotic drip. Do you think you'll be able to keep the IV going for him wherever you're headed?"

The truth was she didn't know, but she'd find a way to make it happen for him. "I'll take care of it."

"Great."

Wendy helped Jagger put on his T-shirt and button-down. They had to go someplace safe, where no one would find them. Give Jagger a chance to recover. A hotel was out of the question. They'd have to use a credit card that could be tracked. There was also the possibility that footage of them from the Lincoln Tunnel had made the news, and so anyone in a crowded hotel might spot them and call the police.

She was glad her mom was safe and out of town with her new husband, Eric. Not that she would have been able to turn to her if she had been in the city. Friends and close associates were out, too.

That left only one place for them to go, and Jagger was going to hate it.

Fitz started the intravenous drip of antibiotics and regular fluids. They attached the IV bag to the top of the backpack after Jagger slipped it on. She would have preferred to carry it for him, but the tubing wasn't long enough.

"Thank you, Fitz," Wendy said. "I appreciate this."

"We're even," he said. "This will never happen again. Right?"

Out of desperation, she'd crossed the line. She felt awful for coercing Fitz. Even though they'd short-circuited the GPS tracker, which gave them a chance to survive, and Jagger was on the mend, the ends didn't justify the means. "Right. Never again."

TWENTY MINUTES LATER, it was nearly eleven thirty.

In the lobby of the Upper East Side apartment building, Wendy smiled at the doorman, who was seated behind the front desk. She had one arm wrapped around Jagger's waist, holding up some of his weight.

"Can't we go somewhere else?" Jagger asked her in an irate whisper.

"No." She turned back at the doorman, pretending that this wasn't a bizarre situation. "We're here to see Tina Jennings."

The doorman's gaze bounced from her, to Jagger, to the IV bag hanging from his backpack. "Is she expecting you?"

"I doubt it unless she's clairvoyant." She broadened her smile.

The doorman showed no reaction to the joke. "Who can I say is calling?"

She wasn't comfortable using their names, but she had to give the man something to work with. "Tell her that Warren's son is here, with his girlfriend."

His eyebrows creased and his eyes narrowed, but he picked up the phone and rang her apartment. He relayed the message, listened briefly, and said. "Yes, ma'am." Rising from his seat, he hung up and looked at them. "You're both welcome to go right up."

He came around the desk, walked to the elevator ahead of them and pushed the button. The doors opened right away, which was a relief. She was ready for this tense, awkward moment to end.

Once she helped Jagger inside, the doorman pushed the button for the top floor.

"Thank you, for the assistance," Wendy said.

He nodded. "Have a good evening."

The doors closed.

"We shouldn't have come here," Jagger said.

"We have nowhere else to go." They were lucky Tina was even letting them come up.

"If it weren't for her stealing my inheritance, none of this would have ever happened. I would've had the money to pay your tuition. You never would have gotten that stupid job. I never would've gone to prison." He grunted in frustration.

"It's time to bury the hatchet. We need someplace safe for you to recover. You said she hasn't had anything to do with the cartel since your father died. Everyone knows how much you—" she swallowed the word *despise* "—dislike her. No one will think to look for us here. We'll leave in the morning."

The elevator doors opened. They walked off and made their way to the apartment.

An elderly woman with a welcoming smile opened the door before Wendy could ring the bell or knock. Her hair was snow-white, her frame thin and a bit frail, but her blue eyes were radiant. She wore a simple cotton blouse and loose-fitting black pants.

Wendy had never met Tina. Jagger had cut ties with her after his father's death. Based on his description, Wendy had assumed his father had been in a May-December relationship with a younger woman. But Tina appeared to be in her late sixties, possibly early seventies, making her Warren Carr's senior by at least ten years.

"Jagger. Come in." She stepped aside, letting them in. After she locked the door and put the chain on, she turned back to them. "Hi, I'm Tina."

Wendy shook her proffered hand. "I'm Wendy."

A curious expression crossed Tina's face. "Wendy Haas?"

"Yes. How did you know?"

"How many Wendys could there be in Jagger's life? When he was on trial, I went to go see him once to offer any assistance I could."

"I asked her to get me a good lawyer," Jagger said, "and she didn't even do that much for me."

"It wasn't that simple." Tina lowered her head. "Jagger shared the details of his case with me. It was a good thing your name was kept out of the paper and you didn't have to worry about reporters hounding you." Tina looked Jagger over from head to toe and frowned. "Why don't you two take a sit?"

The apartment was spacious by Manhattan standards and tastefully decorated. Dark hardwood floors. Comfy-looking leather furniture, also dark. The walls were painted in light, airy neutral colors. There were pictures of Warren everywhere, one with him and Jagger in his military uniform, several of him with Tina.

The place was a shrine.

They shuffled to a sofa and plunked down.

Adrenaline had bled out of Wendy and fatigue was setting in. All she wanted to do was sleep. "We're sorry to intrude on you so late."

"I don't turn in until well after midnight and appreciate the company. I've told Jagger that he's welcome to come here anytime."

"How gracious. I can come to the apartment you stole from me anytime."

Tina pursed her lips and sat in a wingback chair across from them. "To what do I owe this unexpected pleasure?"

"We're in trouble, with the cartel," Wendy said, cutting to the heart of it. Tina had a right to know this if they were going to stay the night.

"Oh, my." Tina blanched. "Is there anything I can do to help?"

"Is this another offer of impotent assistance?" Jagger asked.

Wendy leaned over to Jagger. "Stop it. You're embarrassing yourself and me," she whispered in his ear. "If she kicks us out, you'll have to rest on the subway."

Drawing in a deep breath, Jagger went to fold his arms, but thanks to the tube from the IV, he straightened them instead.

"Could we spend the night?" Wendy asked. "If we had someplace else to go, we wouldn't ask. We'll leave first thing in the morning."

"Of course," Tina said, without expressing any concern for herself or whether she was in danger. "Stay as long as you need."

Wendy's stomach growled in an inconvenient break in the conversation. It was loud and mortifying.

"Can I get you two something to eat?" Tina asked.

Wendy shook her head. "No, thank you. We don't want to impose."

"Yes," Jagger said. "We're starving."

Wendy elbowed his right side lightly.

"Please. Thank you," he added through clenched teeth.

"How about steak and asparagus? And I have an extra baked potato. It can all be ready in ten minutes. Is medium rare all right?"

"That would be lovely," Wendy said, starting to feel a little light-headed from low blood sugar.

"I can also whip up a molten lava cake in the microwave. Homemade, not from a box. It's delicious and gluten-free. I have sugar-free vanilla frozen yogurt to go on top."

"Please don't go to any trouble on our account," Wendy said.

Tina beamed and waved a dismissive hand. "It's been a long time since I've had the pleasure of cooking for anyone. No trouble at all. Why don't I show you two to the guest room?"

"Do you mean my old room?" Jagger asked.

Tina's bright smile faded. "Yes. Your old room."

"I know the way." Jagger stood, and Wendy went to put his arm over her shoulder to help him, but he brushed her away and headed down the hall.

"He's a Carr man, through and through," Tina said in a low voice. "Fortunately, I have a lot of experience. You wipe that pitiful look off your face and go in there after him. I'll let you know when the food is ready."

"Thank you," Wendy said. "I appreciate your kindness."

"Think nothing of it. This is Jagger's home as much as it is mine. He is always welcome here. That's the way Warren would've wanted it."

In the first bedroom down the hall, Wendy found Jagger. He was sitting on the bed, looking drained and irritated, staring at the drawn curtains.

Taking a deep breath, she shut the door behind her and sat beside him. For a long moment, there was only silence between them.

"Hey," she said softly, caressing his face and tilting his gaze to hers. She studied him for a heartbeat. Saw the anger and the pain lurking deeper. "Your father loved you. I love you. Let the rest of it go."

He leaned in and kissed her. A deep, long, melt-her-into-a-puddle kind of a kiss. Breaking away, he put his forehead to hers. He stroked her hair and ran a hand up and down her arm. It was so familiar, so intimate, dragging her back to when they had been together. He used to touch her all the time, always tender, always passionate, like he couldn't keep his hands off her, and it wasn't until that moment she realized how terribly she'd missed his affection.

"If I could let it go, I would," he whispered across her lips. "I can't reconcile what my father did."

Leaving Tina millions when a small portion would've changed Jagger's life. Both their lives.

"It's not Tina's fault. You can be angry, but *mean* is beneath you. You're better than that."

There was more to Jagger Carr than met the eye. She

loved that about him, but she also needed to make sure he remembered that he was a good man, with a big heart. It hurt her to see him like this.

Tina knocked on the door.

"Come in," Wendy said.

The door opened and Tina stepped inside, carrying a coatrack. "I thought this would be handy for the IV bag."

"That's considerate of you." Wendy took it from her and attached the drip bag to one of the hooks.

"The food is ready."

Wendy and Jagger followed her into the dining room off the kitchen. Jagger insisted on carrying the coatrack himself. The color had returned to his face and he was already looking stronger.

Tina plated the meals and set the food down in front of them. As they dug in, she made herself a cup of tea and joined them at the table.

"This is delicious," Wendy said. The steak was tender and juicy, with a buttery texture, and the asparagus was crisp. It hit the spot. "Thank you."

Jagger stuffed food into his mouth, keeping his gaze lowered to the plate.

He'd gone from indignant to mute when she was hoping for cool politeness.

"You look so much like your father," Tina said. "Though you have your mother's eyes."

He responded by clearing his throat and taking a sip of water.

"I'm happy you're here," Tina said, making another attempt at conversation. "The circumstances are regrettable, of course, but I'm always here for you, Jagger."

His gaze slid up to Tina, and hostility rolled off him in waves. "I appreciate that you're allowing us to stay the night, but let's not pretend that we're ever going to be friends."

"Why can't we be friends?" Tina asked in a gentle tone. "What have I done to offend you?"

Jagger set down his fork and knife. "Maybe it has something to do with the fact that my father left you everything."

"No. That's an excuse," Tina said pointedly. "You were like this when your father and I started seeing each other. I have always welcomed you with open arms. Treated you with kindness and respect. I can't say that I've ever received the same in return. I'd like to know why."

Jagger had never shared with Wendy details about his relationship with Tina before his father's death. Everything she'd heard had been colored by the will and his anger over the inheritance.

"You came along at a difficult time for me and my father," Jagger said. "I needed more from him, and everything he had went to the cartel or to you."

"You were the apple of his eye. He loved you more than anything else in this world. More than me."

He laughed in bitter disbelief, and Wendy's heart sank. "Then why did he leave you millions and give me a car and a stupid letter filled with the ramblings of a crazy old man? One hundred thousand dollars to cover her tuition and my life would've had a different trajectory."

It was true. But the same could be said if Wendy had never moved out of the dorm, had never pushed her mother to cut her off. In so many ways she was responsible. Tina wasn't.

Tina rubbed her palms along the side of her mug. "I should've told you this years ago, when I came to see you in jail, but I was embarrassed, and the truth wouldn't have changed anything."

"What truth?" Jagger asked.

"I didn't steal anything from you. Your father didn't leave me millions. His estate owns this apartment. The whole building, in fact. I'm *entitled* to live here, the utilities are paid, and I receive a modest stipend once a month for expenses."

Wendy cringed inwardly as an awkward silence settled around the table like a bad smell. Jagger sat frozen, unblinking. He must have a million questions—she certainly did.

"Who does his estate belong to?" Wendy finally asked when Jagger remained speechless.

"It's in a trust. For Jagger's kids. If he ever has any." Tina's eyes turned glassy. "If he doesn't, then it will go to charity."

Jagger shook his head. "I don't understand. Why wouldn't he leave it to me?" His voice was low, barely audible.

"Your dad knew you so well that he believed you were the type of person who would do better on his own. Top of your class in high school, full scholarship to Columbia University that you turned down to join the army. He never worried about you. Warren so admired you for joining the military and becoming a Ranger. He thought your star would shine brighter if his money didn't influence who you became." She looked down at her cup. "I should've told you that day I came to visit you, but you were so angry at me and I was ashamed that there was nothing I could do to help you. A good lawyer wanted a ten-thousand-dollar retainer. To start with. That's three months of my stipend." She pressed a hand to her cheek. "Whatever I can do to help you now, please let me."

"Why didn't dad's estate planning lawyer explain all of that to me? Why leave me in the dark with a stupid car and that crazy letter about how his legacy would always be there for me, to protect me?"

"I think Warren was trying to be secretive about whatever is inside the Legacy."

"*Inside* the legacy?" Wendy asked. "What do you mean?"

"His safe, that's hidden in the office. It's a Legacy safe. I can show you."

Chapter Seventeen

In his father's office, Tina went to the built-in bookshelf behind the desk. She ran her finger along a seam and hit a button. The upper portion popped loose. She swung the bookcase out, revealing a safe that had been inserted into the wall.

"I never knew there was safe hidden behind the shelf," Jagger said.

"I thought you did." Tina looked at him. "Considering that, other than your father, you're the only person who can open it."

"You're mistaken." How could he open a safe he never knew existed?

"No, I'm not. Warren told me that you could."

"Is it possible your father left a code to unlock it in the letter?" Wendy asked.

He didn't recall any numbers, but the whole letter had been in code. All this time he had thought his father's words didn't make any sense, rambling on about his legacy, when he'd been referring to a safe in his office.

"There's no code. It's a biometric safe." Tina stepped aside, pointing to it. "Your dad was such a long-term planner, always prepared. I'm sure there's a way for you to open it."

Jagger moved closer, carrying the coatrack with the IV bag dangling from a hook. He peered at the safe. There was a biometric fingerprint scanner on the door. Engraved on the top was the brand name, *Legacy*.

A quick burst of nerves sent his pulse skittering.

"Your dad used his thumbprint," Tina said.

His father had used a device to scan Jagger's thumbprint when he was about fourteen or fifteen, but his dad had never deigned to explain why. Since before Jagger had been born, his father had been involved with the cartel. Secrets came with the territory, and at an early age he'd learned to walk on eggshells and follow orders without question. Maybe that was part of the reason he'd made such a good soldier.

Too many secrets and unresolved misunderstandings had brought him here. To this safe. With no clue as to its contents. Had he ever really known his father?

Wendy came up alongside him and put a hand on his back between his shoulder blades, as if sensing he needed support. "You don't have to do this right now. It can wait until the morning, after you've rested."

A trail of hateful little breadcrumbs and a violent shove from fate led him here. To his father's *Legacy*. The prospect of waiting was unbearable. "I have to do this. Now."

He pressed his right thumb to the scanner. A red light on the safe blinked green and the lock disengaged. He pulled the door open.

Inside the safe was a flash drive.

Jagger picked up the USB stick and turned to the computer on the desk. "Do you mind if I use it?"

"Go right ahead. Make yourself at home," Tina said. "Whenever your dad got that same gleam in his eyes, I could tell he was going to pull an all-nighter. Should I put on some coffee?"

"Yes, please," he said.

"No. Thank you." Wendy's gaze shifted to him. "Your heart." She placed her palm on his chest, the gentle heat stirring something tender and bone deep in him. "You need rest. Not caffeine."

As much as he hated to admit it, she was right. When the defibrillator paddles had touched him, it had felt like an electrified mule had kicked his damn chest. He was still fatigued, but curiosity had adrenaline firing through his veins again. "I'll pass on the coffee."

Tina nodded. "I leave you to it then." She headed for the door.

"Wait." Jagger met her eyes. "I'm sorry. For the assumptions I made. For not being nicer to you over the years. You made my dad happy. I should've been grateful to you for that instead of resentful."

"There were times I could've tried harder, too. You were just a kid who wanted more attention from his father. I wish I had encouraged your dad to tell you how he felt about you. He was so guarded about his feelings. Private."

His dad was a tough man, harder on Jagger than any drill sergeant or four-star general. Better at giving an *attaboy* than a hug.

"Don't ever doubt that he loved you." Tina gave him a sad smile and left the room, closing the door.

Jagger sat in front of the computer and turned it on. "I never thought I'd say this, ever, but I feel sorry for Tina. I wasn't fine with her having the bulk of his estate, but for her to only be left with a monthly allowance." He shook his head. That couldn't have been an easy pill to swallow after devoting herself to someone for years. "She deserved better. More."

Wendy kissed the top of his head. "Now that sounds like the man I know and love."

He inserted the thumb drive. "I can't believe my dad didn't want his millions to influence me, but he had no problem turning any children I have into spoiled-rotten brats."

"Isn't that a grandparent's sacred prerogative? Spoil their grandchildren and have their kids clean up the mess. Sort of like feeding them as many homemade cookies as they want, and then sending them back home to their parents to have their sugar rush."

"Well, we're talking ten million dollars' worth of a sweet rush."

"Wow. That's a lot of cookies."

Jagger clicked the folder on the screen for the drive linked to the USB stick. There were multiple files. Holdings. Property, residential and commercial. Every compound and safe house was probably listed. After a quick perusal, he found one in Texas, on the outskirts of El Paso.

"What's that?" Wendy asked, indicating the file labeled Layers.

He opened it and scanned the paperwork. "Documentation on shell companies. These are the layers the cartel uses to hide their money, their drugs, their businesses. It puts distance between them and their illicit activities." If Morton saw this, he'd be drooling right now. "Without the shell companies, they're exposed."

"So this is proof of what they've been doing?"

"If you connect the dots, yes." It was a silver bullet straight to the heart. He opened the next folder called

Accounts. "Do you know how long the feds have been looking for this?"

"Bank accounts. Offshore. Overseas."

"The assets they've been hiding can be frozen with this information. Without money to conduct business as usual, keep the pipeline of drugs flowing, for bribes, it would cut them off at the knees."

"What do you think Transport is?" she asked, pointing to the last folder.

Something his father had once said to him came back. *Transport is the bloodline of the cartel. Their carotid artery. They live or die by it.*

He clicked on the file. "It's a list of the cargo ships they use to transport their drugs in shipping containers. With the names of these vessels, serial numbers and container identifiers, they could be tracked, stopped, searched. Seized. These files show the entire network of Los Chacales. How they transport their drugs, hide their money, the locations of their homes, their safe houses, their properties. This flash drive is the end of the cartel."

She looked up at his IV bag, which was now empty, and removed the needle that had been taped down on his hand. "Are you going to give the thumb drive to Special Agent Morton?"

A part of Jagger wanted to. He'd crush the cartel and have his record expunged, but Morton couldn't save Wendy's life.

Only one thing could.

Jagger went back to the folder of residential properties. He scrolled through until he came across the one in Texas. He'd been to the house in El Paso once, but it had been a long time ago. At first, he thought he might have to recall exactly where it was from memory, but the address was right here in front of him. "Going to Morton is the wrong play. We need to go Texas."

"Why?"

"To see Emilio."

Wendy reeled back, her eyes wide, her mouth open in shock. "You *are* insane. The chicken doesn't pay the fox a visit."

Jagger wasn't a chicken, or a fox. He was a wolf. Trained by jackals and the US Army. "I always knew there were two ways for this blood debt to end. You die or Emilio dies, but I couldn't get to him because he was in jail. Thanks to his little prison break he's not anymore."

"You want to try to kill him?"

"No." Not now that he had these files. "I want to negotiate. Your life and mine for this information."

"The FBI already has Emilio on kidnapping charges that aren't going away, probably a life sentence according to the news. Why would he care about these files?"

"Because of his legacy. If I hand this over to him instead of the FBI, it'll keep his only son, Miguel, out of prison, and the Los Chacales stay in power in North America. This file in FBI hands means no safe houses for him, no money for the cartel, no power while he's in prison. He'll negotiate."

"What if he doesn't agree?"

"Then I'll kill him."

"Do you hear yourself?" She sat on the edge of the desk and cupped his face in her hands. "This isn't logical."

Love wasn't logical. It made people crazy. Made them do beautiful things. Terrible things that they wouldn't otherwise. And Jagger would do anything to protect Wendy. "It's the only way."

"We can go to Special Agent Morton. He gets his win and you get your record expunged. The cartel loses power and I stay safe. Then we get our second chance."

Jagger wanted that more than anything, a clean slate and to be with Wendy, but that might not be possible. "There's a blood debt, Wendy. That won't magically disappear. Emilio can be apprehended and sent back to jail. Miguel can be arrested, brought up on charges based on these files, and that blood debt will still exist. The Brethren will seek to carry it out. They will honor it if it's the last thing they do. You'll be looking over your shoulder for the rest of your life. Is that what you want? To know your days are numbered and to spend them waiting for a *sicario* to show up?"

She dropped her hands from his face. "Stop it."

"Because they're going to keep coming until you're dead."

"I said stop." She stood and moved away, but he caught her wrist.

As individual hit men, each person in the Brethren was formidable, but the whole was greater than the sum of its parts. United, they were a terrifying force, and they would honor the code of the blood debt.

"This is the only way. Emilio rescinds the kill order. Or he dies." He got up from the chair and brought her into his arms. "If Morton was a realistic option to keep you alive, I'd take it."

"Witness protection. That's realistic."

"You'll never make it into the program." He nudged her chin up with finger, forcing her to look at him. "Do you know how many steps there are, how long it'll take? The information on the flash drive would put an end to the cartel, but it'd be a slow death. Months, years of red tape in the legal system just to have a trial. Los Chacales won't go down without a fight. Feds will die. Prosecutors will have accidents. Their families will be terrorized and threatened. While that's happening, the Brethren will find you, they'll find *us*, before Emilio or Miguel ever see the inside of a courtroom."

"I don't like it."

"If it's any consolation, neither do I." He also couldn't escape the certainty that this was the right course of action, the one he was always meant to take.

A call to serve led him to become an army Ranger, trained to do precisely what he was proposing. A direct-action raid in a hostile environment to kill a high-value target. Or, if he got lucky, negotiate. His history with the cartel, his father's legacy, was the only thing giving him the chance to pull it off. Out of all the US Marshals who had to seduce Isabel Vargas and persuade her to betray Emilio, it ended up being Dutch Haas.

This was a serious alignment of planets. A once-in-a-lifetime grand trine, but whether the end result of this conjunction would be positive or negative was anyone's guess.

Wendy slid her hands up his chest and linked them behind his neck. "I want you to be safe instead of risking yourself for me again."

"There is one unbreakable moral line above anything else for men like Emilio. Protect your children, no matter the cost." That was why his own father had left him those files. "I can get him to agree to a deal. I know I can." If he was wrong, then he'd put a bullet in Emilio. "I know where I need to go in El Paso, I just don't know how to get there. It's not like I can fly, and that'll be two to three days in a car."

"Are you sure about this?"

He brushed his knuckles across her cheek. "I am."

"Then I might be able to help."

"How?"

"My newest client is Chase Rothersbury. He happens to own a private plane, or rather his family does. That means bypassing TSA, no ID check and no baggage search. We've signed the contract, but I haven't been paid yet. Maybe he'll let us use his plane as payment."

"Us?"

"Wherever you go, I go. You're not leaving me behind."

Getting her out of New York was probably safer anyway, and flying private would be ideal. He wouldn't have to leave any of his gear behind. "Okay." He brushed his lips across hers. She leaned back in his arms, her softness yielding to him, but he didn't mistake her soft body or concession for weakness. She was the most determined, headstrong woman he'd ever met. "Do you think this Rothersbury might help?"

"There's only one way to find out. I'll make the call and ask."

Chapter Eighteen

Wendy held the receiver of the landline phone to her ear. "Chase, thank you for agreeing to this. I know allowing me to use your family's plane instead of paying me is an irregular arrangement."

"It's a win-win. My parents will foot the bill and I'll reap the benefits."

"I appreciate your discretion," she said. It was a done deal. Despite the horror of the past few hours, a smile pulled at her mouth and entered her voice. "I'll be at the hangar at noon sharp and will give your pilot the exact destination then." She had to give him a city within a hundred miles to file the flight plan, but Jagger didn't want Chase or anyone for that matter to know where they were going until they were in the air.

There was a knock at the door and Tina hurried into the office. "You're on TV," she whispered. "The authorities have identified you from the incident in the Lincoln Tunnel, but they still don't know who Jagger is."

Wendy swore at the timing. Then again, this gave her a chance to manage it. "Chase, before you go, I need you to turn on the news for a moment."

"What for?"

"There's something you should see."

Jagger stood. *What are you doing?* he mouthed.

She covered the receiver. "He's going to find out. It's better to face it now." Over the line, she heard the television in the background.

"Wendy, I'm speechless," Chase said. "As my mother can attest, that's rare."

"I haven't done anything illegal, but the authorities have questions for me." She deliberately made no mention of Jagger. "In twenty-four hours, the optics will have changed."

"Hmm."

With that being his only response, she wished she saw precisely what was being reported.

"I'm no longer comfortable with our arrangement," Chase said. "My current predicament is bad enough as is." A second DUI and property damage in the Hamptons. "I came to you to make it better. Not worse."

"Not helping me will only hurt you."

"How do you figure?"

"You chose me out of the other PR firms for a reason. Do you remember what that was?"

"Everyone else wanted me to hide behind the Rothersbury coattails and do community service. You saw more than my bloodline. You saw me and had great ideas to reform me in the public eye. Your proposal was nothing short of electrifying."

She hadn't even gotten into the nuts and bolts of how she would do it. During a proposal, you had to be impressive without giving the cow away for free. "I'm going to make you a household name. A role model who will inspire young people. Others can learn from your mistakes. You're going to glamourize clean living, a healthy state of mind, supporting the environment." Putting his name and money to worthwhile causes. If other celebrities could get DUIs, resist arrest, assault a police officer and turn that into a popular cabaret show, everything she promised Chase was more than feasible. "I'm going to make you an influencer. I'll be working on rebuilding your image even while you're in rehab."

"That all sounds great, but—"

"I have a contact who is willing to collaborate with you on a mobile app." It was a booming sector of the tech business that Chase was keen to enter, but his profile as a bad boy was toxic and no one wanted to take a chance on him. "A well-known video game developer. I convinced him that you're perfect for the project, but you'll have to give up your old circle of friends. Consider it a gesture of goodwill that you're serious."

"Isn't rehab a gesture?"

"No. That's court mandated. You'll have some creative input, and I can set up a preliminary meeting before you leave for rehab." It was the biggest carrot she had to dangle. If he didn't bite, they'd have to drive to Texas. "You have very little to lose and everything to gain. What do you say?"

"Okay, but to reduce my risk you leave in three hours. There's hardly any personnel at the Westchester airport at that time, and because the on-call flight crew will get paid time and a half they'll gladly turn a blind eye."

"Sounds good. Thanks." She hung up and looked between Jagger and Tina. "We're taking a red-eye flight."

"That's so soon," Tina said, "but it's probably for the best. The doorman won't say anything about you two. A resident, on the other hand, will call the police in a heartbeat. It'll be easier for you to slip out of the building unseen in the middle of the night."

"Are you sure the cops won't be waiting for us at the airport?"

"Chase has been living in his family's shadow his entire life. The spotlight has only been on him for negative press. Another PR firm can deflect the dirt for a little while with community service photo ops, but I'm the only one who is offering him a way to carve his own path. Not to hide what he's done wrong, but to use it to change the narrative to his benefit."

She was worried about Chase relapsing down the road, but the more invested he was in himself, with things like the mobile app, blogging about his journey—another one of her ideas—forcing him to take public accountability of his lifestyle choices, the better his odds for success.

"He likes my proposal," she said. "Likes the person that he can become with my plan. Calling the cops on me isn't going to turn him into a hero or give him what he wants. Deep down, he knows that."

"Okay," Jagger said.

"I want you to get some rest. We'll leave in two hours."

"You could use a nap, too. Why don't you come lie down with me?" He pulled her close, wrapping his arms around her.

Tina excused herself with a coy smile, closing the door.

Jagger kissed Wendy, really kissed her as he ran his hands down her back and to her hips. Hot and deep and full of need. A familiar hunger burned through her, racing over her skin.

This was everything she wanted and not enough, at the same time. She loved the feel of his lips, the taste of him, the way he touched her with the right mix of tenderness and roughness.

Her plus Jagger together in bed wouldn't equal rest. Kissing, touching, him inside her... She'd thought about it. Wanted him, craved him. Pictured him when she closed her eyes. Remembered the intoxicating pleasure and knowing without a doubt that she belonged with him.

But he was planning to go up against the head of a cartel and had to be at the top of his game, needed his strength.

She eased back. "You died a couple of hours ago. You need to sleep."

"I didn't die. My heart stopped for a second. There was no tunnel. No bright white light. And I still felt you with me."

He owned a piece of her that she prayed would always be with him. In this life and the next.

"Don't fight me on this because you'll lose. If you want to face Emilio, you need to get your strength back. I'm glad Fitz thought to give you the IV, but you also need rest. As much as possible for the next—" she glanced at the clock "—ten hours. Doctor's orders."

"Yes, ma'am." He kissed her nose. "What are you going to do?"

"I need to email my game developer contact and get the ball rolling for Chase." In the event of a worst-case scenario, she wanted to make good on her promises and have Chase poised for success. "Then I'll catch a few winks on the sofa."

"Want to tuck me in?" He waggled his eyebrows, but she saw the fatigue in his eyes.

Smiling, she hauled him into the hallway. "Not a good idea, mister." She nudged him in the direction of the guest room. "Rest."

"Will do." After another kiss, he disappeared into the bedroom, shutting the door.

She went back to the desk and sent the email to the video game developer.

Her gaze fell back to the files on the thumb drive. The folders were still up on the screen.

Even if the negotiation with that madman panned out, they should have copies of the information. What if Emilio decided to double-cross them later? Jagger believed in the code of the cartel, but she didn't trust any of those jackals.

She right clicked on the main folder. The total size of all the documents were over a hundred megabytes. An email attachment supported twenty-five megs. It wasn't as sleek and sexy as having a duplicate flash drive but emailing herself copies of the folders would suffice.

The only problem was if Emilio killed them both, how would justice be served?

Jagger's plan was dangerous, and a million things could go wrong.

The cocktail of hormones and adrenaline must have dulled her common sense if she was going along with this. Not that he'd back down.

When Jagger made up his mind, there was no changing it.

It wasn't that she didn't think he couldn't pull it off—she knew he was capable, had witnessed it firsthand tonight. He backed up his confidence with lethal action. Put himself in the line of fire and protected her again and again.

Maybe it was time for her to protect him. If only she knew how.

Picking up the landline, she punched in her brother's

cell phone number. Once again it went straight to voice mail and the box was full. She still couldn't leave a message.

Dutch, where in the hell are you?

Her brother would drop everything to help her, if only he knew she needed him.

Wendy got up and left the office. She tiptoed down the hall past Jagger's room and found Tina in the living room, watching the news.

"Any more updates?" Wendy asked.

"No. They're clueless as to Jagger's identity." Tina stared at her a moment. "I don't think anyone will recognize you with that black hair."

Wendy had forgotten about the hair dye spray. As soon as she showered, it would be gone. "I know we've asked a lot of you tonight already, but I'd like to trouble you for one more favor."

"Sure. What is it?"

"Jagger and I are going to El Paso to negotiate with Emilio Vargas. There's a chance that things could go sideways."

"Emilio is dangerous. Warren always treaded with care around him. They seemed to have an understanding, but to this day I wonder if Emilio is the reason my Warren died in Venezuela. I traveled with him on his business trips all the time. That's the reason I didn't work while we were together. I had to be able to pick up and go at a moment's notice. But he didn't want me to go to Venezuela."

"Did Emilio go on that trip?"

"Yes, I believe so."

"Does Jagger know?"

Tina shrugged. "We really weren't on speaking terms

when Warren died. It was a tough time." She took a framed picture of Warren from the side table and stared at it with fondness in her eyes. "What was the favor, dear?"

"Oh, I wanted to email you a copy of the files we found on the thumb drive. If you don't hear from us in two days, I'd like you to send the documents to my brother. I'll include his email address and phone number in the body of the message."

Wendy could have simply sent the files straight to Dutch right now, but if Jagger managed to pull a white rabbit out of his bag of tricks and Emilio agreed to the deal, her brother would act on the information and the truce would be null and void.

Tina reached over and took her hand. Her skin was paper-thin and soft as cotton, but warm. "I'll do it. For you. For Jagger. For Warren."

"Thank you."

"I do have one request in return. If you two make it through this and come out on the other side, I'd like to see Jagger. At least once a year. A day of his choosing, though I'm partial to the anniversary of Warren passing."

Tina didn't have to say it, the loneliness in her face spoke volumes. No husband, no children. All she had were these pictures, memories and a connection to the man she'd loved through Jagger.

"I'll make sure he visits."

"You'll come, too?" Tina patted her hand. "You seem to have a calming effect on him."

Wendy laughed. "We'll both come visit." And they could do better than once a year.

First, they had to survive.

Chapter Nineteen

On the patio of his safe house, Emilio turned his face up to the Texas sun and stretched after his long nap. Basked in the warm light and the fresh air as a free man. He gazed out at the vast Chihuahuan Desert surrounding the property. Many people assumed that Texas was a hot, dry, barren region, but this was shrub desert, sprinkled with grasses, where many things thrived. The rocky landscape was dotted with cacti and yuccas and agaves, the Guadalupe Mountains not far in the distance.

He loved El Paso. Plenty of space for privacy, and he could count on the sun shining for three hundred days out of the year. That was more than San Diego by double.

There was nothing much around for miles. Set fifty feet from his house were three trailers. Two were for his men. Room for them to unwind and sleep. To bring women for a little fun when they got bored.

The third was reserved for a special purpose.

There was the clack of cowboy boots across the wood floors, growing louder, coming his way. "Lunch is ready, Don Emilio," Samuel said, stepping outside.

"I wish to eat here in the open air."

Behind him, Samuel snapped his fingers and spoke

hurriedly to the cooking staff. Dishes and glasses clinked. There was the distinct ting of silverware being set.

"As you wish," Samuel said. "Everything is prepared."

Emilio spun on his heel and looked over the table. Lobster salad with roasted corn. A champagne flute had been set out along with a bottle of Krug Grande Cuvée in a bucket of ice.

His mouth watered as he sat. "Take away the champagne. I'll drink it after I have Special Agent Maximiliano Webb shackled in that trailer." He pointed to the third one. "Receiving his punishment for his betrayal."

Samuel beckoned to one of the cooks, who stood by waiting to make sure everything was up to snuff. "Remove the champagne. Bring him a Scotch."

Good lieutenants who anticipated his desires were hard to find.

The young woman bowed her head, came around the table, and took away the champagne and flute.

"You'll have Max soon. He'll be here tonight."

"Excellent." Emilio took a bite of lobster. The sweet, tender meat practically melted in his mouth. Cooked to perfection. He would've invited Samuel to join him, but that was the mistake he'd made in the past with other lieutenants. Allowed them to get too close. Permitted the line between professionalism and friendship to blur.

That's what burned him down the marrow of his bone. Not only had he trusted Max, but also he thought of the man as a friend. A confidant.

"I want him to suffer," Emilio said. "Make it slow and painful, but when I'm finally ready to kill him, I want him to be conscious enough to know that I'm the one pulling the trigger."

Delicate business keeping a prisoner alive and aware

through hours of torture. It needed to be planned with care and executed with finesse. He had the utmost confidence in Samuel's skills.

"*Sí*, Don Emilio. It will be done."

The young woman returned, carrying a bottle of Scotch. Thirty-year-old Isle of Jura. His favorite. She set the bottle on the table and Samuel poured his drink.

Emilio swirled the amber liquid in his crystal tumbler. Inhaled the scent of vanilla and guava and toasted oak. He sipped it, letting the full-bodied flavors roll over his tongue. Moaning his satisfaction, he smiled. Everything tasted better after being released from captivity.

He pierced a fat piece of lobster on his fork and was about to savor another bite when Samuel's cell phone rang.

"It's Pilar Zahiri. She called while you were sleeping. She wanted to speak with you directly, but I told her you gave orders not to be disturbed."

Pilar. Intelligent. Beautiful. Deadly. Loyal. Everything he wanted in a daughter-in-law. She'd be the perfect mate for Miguel. His equal. Perhaps even his son's better in some ways.

Lowering the fork, he extended his other hand for the phone. "Yes, Pilar," he said, as one of his other bodyguards came outside, whispered in Samuel's ear, and passed him another phone.

Samuel stepped away, taking the call.

"Don Emilio, you're awake. Good. I'm calling with news. I found out why Jagger Carr is protecting the woman."

If anyone could, it was her. "Tell me, my dear. Apparently, you're the only one capable. My men are still in the dark about Jagger."

"That's because they've been looking in the wrong place. Digging into his present when they should've been looking into his past."

"As titillating as you make the suspense, my patience is thin."

"Wendy Haas is the reason Jagger went to prison. She was the woman he was living with at the time. The one he got into a fight over and killed a man."

At the time of Jagger's trial, her name hadn't been mentioned in the newspaper and Jagger had never discussed the incident with anyone in the cartel to his knowledge.

"How can you be certain?"

"I saw him last night," Pilar said. "He came to me desperate for help and spilled his guts. We fought. I injured him, but he got away."

Emilio picked up his glass and took a gulp of Scotch. The sweet burn slid down his throat, taking the chill away from his belly. Jagger had already gone to prison once for the woman. There was no way he was going to throw her to the jackals.

Jagger Carr had drawn a line in the sand.

"Is there anything else, my dear?"

There was a pause. A long, deliberate pause because Pilar never did anything by accident. Every move, every word, was calculated. The way she was able to think on her feet was astounding.

"No, Don Emilio. I only wish to be of service."

Pilar was young, but she understood what it took many others a lifetime to learn. The people who were useful and could do something for you got respect, curried favor, and the ones who were useless lost it.

He had no time for useless things. Or people.

"You have been. Good job." He disconnected and handed the phone back to Samuel.

The pause from her taunted him. She wanted to say more, but hadn't. Perhaps she was concerned about Jagger. They had once been close friends.

Friends were a liability in this business. Most of the time. There were always rare exceptions. Emilio missed Warren. The one true friend he had and considered to be like family. That man had stuck with him through the highs and lows, thick and thin. They didn't make them like Warren anymore.

It was a shame he was going to have to kill his son.

Samuel finished his phone call and took a seat. "That was Alaric. Late last night they lost the signal on Jagger's GPS tracker. They're not sure why. No one has confirmed a kill. They were hoping his body would turn up in a morgue." Samuel shook his head. "No luck. It's still possible that he's dead."

That would be too convenient.

Emilio didn't like it. Something was off about the situation. Not the least of which was that both Pilar and Alaric had waited hours to update him. "It's also possible that Jagger figured out somehow that we were tracking him and found a way to neutralize the signal." Emilio never underestimated someone's will to survive. "Tell the others to assume Jagger Carr is alive and when they find him, he's fair game."

JAGGER HAD PARKED the beater vehicle they'd rented using cash behind a rocky mound.

Looking through the binoculars, he watched Emilio Vargas eating on his patio. The man had just broken out of prison and was dining on lobster and drinking Scotch, the good stuff, like he was on vacation at a resort.

It was too bad Jagger didn't have the training or proper rifle to be a sniper. This range was doable. They were less than twelve hundred yards away.

Security was light. Five bodyguards. Two vehicles. A couple of household staff.

Sweat rolled off his forehead. It was hotter than Hades. The temperature had climbed to record-breaking ninety and he couldn't wait for the sun to go down for multiple reasons.

He lowered the binoculars. "Are you clear on the plan?"

"We'll come back after nightfall. I'll hang back here while you go do your Ranger thing, taking out the men in the trailers and around the perimeter first. If I see anyone coming up behind you," she said, and tapped the package of Bluetooth intercom earpieces they'd purchased in the El Paso airport, "I've got you covered and I'll let you know. Once you're in the house, you're on your own."

"I'll ditch the earpiece inside. I don't want Emilio to know I'm communicating with anyone. No matter what happens, once I'm in the house, you do not follow me in."

Wendy nodded.

"Honey, I need to hear you say it."

"I won't follow you inside. I promise. No matter what."

"Don't forget to remain aware of your surroundings. There are mountain lions, snakes and other predators in the area."

"As long as there are no jackals, I'll be okay."

He kissed her forehead. "We've got eight hours to kill. Let's get out of here."

They climbed into the old pickup truck, and he eased away from the spot he'd scouted.

He turned the truck around and went at a slow speed, twenty miles per hour. More of a crawl. It helped prevent kicking up dust in the air as they drove away, which would draw dangerous attention. The rocky terrain helped mask their leaving the area, but he needed to do all he could to maintain the element of surprise.

"I really owe Chase Rothersbury one," Wendy said.

"He came through. I guess you're pretty good at reading people."

"I have to be for my job."

He finally reached the main road and pressed down on the gas pedal. They zipped off along the asphalt. "I always pictured you at some high-powered PR firm. How were you able to start your own company and compete with the big dogs?"

"So you don't know everything about me." Wendy smiled. "I was at a big, high-powered company for a while. I'd built up my client list and was starting to make a name for myself. One of the partners invited me to dinner at a restaurant in a hotel to discuss my future. I went. Like an idiot."

Jagger tightened his hands on the steering wheel. "He put the moves on you?"

"He did. His approach was very transactional. If I slept with him, I would do well. If I didn't, I would never advance. *The choice is yours*, he'd said to me."

"Did you slap him? Throw a knee to his groin."

"No, Jagger. Although, sometimes when I think back on it, I wish I had been brave enough to throw a drink in his face."

"You are brave. Don't ever let some idiot make you think otherwise." He took her hand and squeezed. "What did you do?"

"I quit and took a couple of clients with me. About week later, a different partner came to see me. The only woman in the firm. She knew what I had been through without me telling her the story, and she didn't share many details of what had happened to her. After she apologized for not being a mentor to me, she informed me that she had threatened the other partners. If they invoked the noncompete clause in my contract, which would've made me liable for taking those two clients, she was going round up all the women they'd harassed and encourage them to file a lawsuit. Then she offered me seed money to start my own company. She's my silent partner. From time to time, she floats clients my way, ones that would be a better fit for a young progressive than the other firm."

"It took courage to quit and go out on your own. I'm proud of you. You're a trailblazer."

A blush rose to her creamy cheeks. "Thanks, but she's the reason I was able to make it and become so successful so fast."

"You're the person who puts in the hard work and convinces clients to sign on the dotted line. You made your company a success."

He turned into the small motel off the I-10 Interstate, outside the city, where they'd gotten a room. Forty bucks a night. Unlike Manhattan, here they could pay cash and leave a little extra for incidentals. Nobody cared and no one questioned that they didn't use a credit card.

Parking in front of their room, he shut off the engine. She unlocked the room door while he gathered up their gear.

"Next time we go out, it'll be dark. Do you think it's okay if I wash this dye out of my hair? Every time I touch the stuff, it gets on my fingers."

"It should be fine," he said, dumping everything on the desk. "When we leave, wear your hair up and put the ball cap on." He wiped sweat from his forehead with the back of his hand. "I'll shower after you. Feel free to use as much hot water as you need."

A cold shower would do him good. Since they had been at Tina's, he'd been thinking about tearing off Wendy's clothes. Touching her on the bed. Making love to her on the plane. Even when they'd first arrived at the motel in El Paso, but she'd been more focused on the mission than he was.

Ten minutes under the cold spray of water would reset his mind.

Wendy kicked off her shoes and pulled her top overhead, revealing her lace bra. "Or you could join me?"

"In the shower?"

A ghost of a smile curved her lips and she stepped backward into the bathroom. "Yeah." She turned on the water and her gaze returned to his. "We used to shower together all the time. Remember?"

More like make love together in the shower all the time because he couldn't control himself being within reach of her naked body, with water sluicing over her curves. Getting her soapy and clean, just to have the pleasure of dirtying her up again, had been…irresistible.

How could he ever forget? "I remember."

She unzipped her jeans, slid them down her hips, past her thighs and took them off.

His gaze toured over the swell of her breasts, down her slim waist, to her shapely thighs and back up to her face. "You're still the most enticing woman I've ever seen."

"Is that a yes?"

"No," he said, and her smile faltered. "That's a *hell*, yes."

WENDY HELD OUT her hand to Jagger and he went to her without hesitation. She tugged his shirt off and said, "Let me look at you a minute."

Even with excitement blazing in his eyes and his fingers twitching from his crumbling control, he stood still. There were times she used to tease him with her fingers and mouth until he was a quivering, begging mess. That's what they did, gave their bodies to each other. With complete trust.

She took in the sight of him, let her hands explore his chest. Strong, sculpted, solid, thicker with muscle than before. Gently she traced around the wound on his side. "Are you going to be okay if we do this?"

His heavy breathing filled the heated air between them. "I'll be better than okay. Probably the best I've ever been. Trust me."

She reached for his belt, struggled to unclasp the buckle, and unzipped his jeans. "Condoms?"

"I picked some up in the airport when we got the earpieces."

"I missed that. You're sly." She slipped her hand inside his pants, palmed his growing erection in one hand and felt the hammering of his heart under the other pressed to his chest.

A husky growl rumbled in his throat, and it was the sexiest sound, spurring her on.

"I'm not sly, I'm just always prepared," he said, and whipped out a condom from his pocket.

"Indeed, you are." This was the quiet before the storm. Their chance to love each other. To be bold and honest. Not hold anything back. "I want you."

When his lips touched hers, she sighed, melting against him. His hand cupped her breast, tugging down the front of her bra, and he dragged his thumb over her nipple. A needy sound from the back of her throat spilled from her lips into his mouth.

Easing away, he looked down at her and licked his lips. He unhooked her bra, letting it fall to the floor. She glanced at her bare chest. The tight, rosy points of her breasts declaring how aroused she was made her cheeks heat.

Smiling, he gripped the thin waistband of her panties and pulled it down.

On his way back up, he shed his jeans and boxer briefs and showered her legs with kisses and licks and nibbles. His eyes finally met hers. "You're so beautiful I can barely stand it."

She dragged him into the shower under the warm spray of water. A thrill rushed through her.

"Hang on." He grabbed the tiny bottle of shampoo, poured some in his hand and worked up a thick lather in her hair. Massaging her scalp with slow, sensuous strokes, he made her whole her body soften.

He put her back under the water and rinsed her hair. He brought his soapy hands to her shoulders and rubbed them, skimming his fingers over her throat, down her back, up to her breasts.

All of it was more intimate than sex somehow and required a level of vulnerability she'd never had with anyone else.

Turning, she ran her hands up his chest, brought his head down and kissed the hell out of him.

Their hands roamed over each other, her body sliding against his in the water.

"I want you inside me?" she whispered.

"Where do you want me? Here." His thumb skimmed

her lips, dipping into her mouth, and she sucked his finger. "Or…" His hand drifted down her body, caressing every inch along the way, and his fingers slipped between her thighs, diving inside her while hers stroked the thick length of him. "Here?"

"Do I have to pick and choose?" she asked around a needy whimper.

"I would never be that selfish."

She laughed, he laughed, and they kissed. She'd missed this. The affection and the fun. How playful they'd been together. His mouth, that tongue, his hands, his chest pressed to hers.

Their attraction was visceral, the heat building around them like a cocoon. The rest of the world disappeared. Nothing else existed but the two of them, locked together in that bittersweet moment, and she wished the sun would never set.

Chapter Twenty

A dark thrill coursed through Emilio as he stood in the trailer reserved for his guest. "Special Agent Maximiliano Webb."

With his hands and ankles handcuffed to a steel chair that had been bolted to the floor, Max stared at him. His long hair had been shorn. His beard was gone, and his face was clean-shaven. He looked like Samson after he lost his strength. A different man. Of course, that was the point. Once he finished a deep cover assignment, the FBI would want him to change his appearance.

Max's face was bruised, bottom lip split, knuckles bloody from fighting back.

He was still in fairly good condition, barely harmed, but Emilio's men were just getting started.

"Don Emilio," Max said.

"Still you use the title of respect for me. Why?"

"Respect?" Max spit blood onto the floor. "For me, don means scumbag, miscreant, swine. And those are some of the kinder definitions."

"I'm above the law, Maximiliano. Haven't you learned that by now?"

"No one is above the law."

"Yet, here I stand. Free. On American soil. I didn't

crawl through a tunnel back into Mexico like a rat trying to escape a sinking ship." Emilio shoved his hands
into the pockets of his linen pants. "While you are in *my*
trailer. Chained like an animal to *my* chair. And before
you die, you will know *my* brand of justice in excruci-
ating detail."

"You've got it all planned out, huh?"

"As a matter of fact, I do. After you're dead, I'll track
down your loved ones and make them suffer, too. Your
ex-wife and your son."

"They're not a part of this." Max struggled against
the handcuffs like he wanted to tear Emilio to bits with
his bare teeth.

"You made them a part of this. By gambling, playing
against me instead of for me. Don't get upset when the
house wins. And the house always wins."

"That's all you understand. Violence. Anger. Revenge.
Isn't it?"

"I do know these things, intimately." His life had been
hard, and if he had not become a brutal man capable
of unspeakable horrors, he wouldn't have survived. A
man like Max would never understand the things Emilio
had survived, endured, so he would not waste his time
or breath explaining it. "I also know love and joy and
mercy."

"Yet, you still lost Isabel because she saw you for the
monster that you really are."

His heart suddenly felt brittle and squeezed painfully
in his chest. His mind shouted at him to silence Max with
a bullet, but he would not be overcome with rage. Instead
he would take pleasure in this man's punishment.

"If you so much as whisper her name again," Emilio
said softly, "I will have them cut out your tongue."

There was a flicker of something in Max's eyes—fear, panic, Emilio couldn't be sure. Whatever it was, he very much liked seeing it.

"You may think you have a monopoly on justice and that you're above the law," Max said, "but karma is coming for you. It's just a matter of time."

A smug smile tugged at Emilio's mouth. "When my men are done hurting you, I will come back to send you on your way to hell." Pivoting on his heel, he moved toward the door.

"Do you hear that?" Max asked.

Emilio glanced at him over his shoulder. "Hear what?"

"Ticktock."

Emilio felt his smile slip away as his jaw hardened. A cold niggle of dread stirred in his belly, but he quickly dismissed it. "Soon the only thing you'll hear is the sound of your own screams."

JAGGER HANDED WENDY the binoculars. "Emilio is heading back inside the house."

"There's a lot more activity than earlier."

"Two more vehicles showed up. Extra men. By my count there are now ten."

He laid out all the weapons from his pack on the hood of the truck. After taking inventory for the third time, he geared up. Two 9 mm guns with silencers went into holsters. Extra loaded magazines and his garrote were in his pockets. He had already rigged a detonator to six ounces of C-4, to be able to use it quickly.

The timing of when he set it off had to be right, because once it blew everyone would know he was there, and the element of surprise would be lost.

The last smoke grenade he stuffed into a utility pocket

of the cargo pants he'd picked up at a thrift store near their motel.

After he attached the sound suppressor to his Heckler & Koch MP5 submachine gun, he slipped the strap over his head and one shoulder. It was too bad he didn't have his sophisticated laser sight. Wendy had done the best she could, packing in a hurry. He was lucky to have this much gear.

Jagger picked up his switchblade. He pushed the release button and the blade flashed out with a harsh metallic click. Flipping the knife in his palm, he handed it to Wendy, handle first.

She took knife and hit the button, retracting the blade.

"Please take one of the guns," he said, wishing he had the shotgun to leave her.

"No, you'll need them. I'll be way back here, safe."

"The wildlife in the area can be dangerous. Maybe you should wait in the truck. Or better yet, go back to the motel."

Her beautiful eyes gleamed with stubbornness. "I'm not leaving you. And I'm not staying in the truck. I won't be able to see the house, and the very least I can do is cover your back."

"What are you going to do if you see a mountain lion?"

"Stay away from it."

"What if it doesn't stay away from you?"

She hit the button on the knife and the blade glinted in the moonlight. "Satisfied?"

Hardly. Shaking his head, he went around to the back of the truck and pulled out the emergency road kit. When he'd checked it earlier, he'd seen a flare gun. Not uncommon to have one out here in the desert in case you got stranded.

He handed her the flare gun. "It'll scare off a preda-tor, but if you get into trouble, tell me."

A beat of hesitation. "Okay, I will," she said, and he knew she was lying.

"I won't be able to focus if I'm worried about you. That's the kind of distraction that could get me killed. I need to trust that you'll tell me."

It was a test of sorts. If she lied again, he was hauling her back to the motel and duct taping her to a chair until this was done. She'd hate it. He'd hate doing it. But she'd be safe, and that was all that mattered to him. The thought of her in danger sent his heart into free fall every time.

She brushed her thumb over his forehead, down the side of his face, rubbed his bottom lip, and his brain mis-fired, his thoughts careening back to the motel room, under the water with her, in the bed, falling asleep with his arms wrapped around her, holding her as close as possible. Feeling like they were one again.

What was she doing to him? Turning him to mush when he needed to steel himself for battle.

"You owe me more kisses and showers, and I intend to collect," she said, her voice firm and sure. "So, put your mind at ease. If I'm in trouble, you'll know."

He believed her.

She handed him his earpiece and put hers in.

He pulled her to him, needing to kiss her, but she put her fingertips up to his mouth.

"After," she said, and he thought back to being in the ambulance, preparing to die. "For now, get your head in the game, soldier." She shoved back, slid the knife into her pocket, put the flare gun on the hood and grabbed the binoculars.

She. Was. Right.

His sole focus had to be getting to Emilio. The man was going to cancel the blood debt or Jagger would kill him, effectively putting an end to it anyway. Either way worked for him.

He headed out in a slow jog under the cover of darkness and didn't look back. "Testing. One. Two. Three."

"I've got you loud and clear," she said, her voice husky in his ear.

He used the terrain to mask his approach. Quick and quiet, he stayed low, dropping to the ground when necessary, using the shrubs as concealment. The wind whistled across the land. Noises grew louder the closer he got. People talking. Music playing somewhere. He crept up to one of the trailers without incident and peeked through a break in the curtains.

A guard was inside with a young woman Jagger had seen earlier in the house. She was sitting on his lap with a look of disgust, which didn't stop the guy from touching her.

"The door to the first trailer closest to the house just opened," Wendy said.

Jagger crouched low, pressing up against the side of the third trailer.

"A man left. He's walking into the house. One of the guards out front followed him inside, but two guards are still patrolling the perimeter."

He didn't respond verbally, not wanting to alert anyone that he was there, but gave her a thumbs-up.

"I see you," she said, as if reading his mind.

Jagger pressed on to the next trailer. A radio was playing. The lyrics were Spanish. Three men were sitting around drinking beer and playing cards.

He put the C-4 against the wall where the sofa was on

the other side. This would kill three birds with one stone, but he didn't set the timer, leaving it set to explode with a manual trigger. He had the detonator tucked away close.

Drawing the MP5 up at the ready, he darted to the last trailer, the one closest to the house. Unlike the others, there were no windows. He had no idea how many men were inside, but he made out the sound of flesh hitting flesh. Grunts of pain interlaced with profanity.

The only door faced the house. That meant he'd have to take out the two guards on patrol first and hope no one spotted their dead bodies before he detonated the C-4.

He edged around the side of the trailer and sneaked a quick glance.

One guard was vigilant, his head on a swivel, his rifle in his hands. The other was smoking, and had his weapon slung over his shoulder. As soon as the wary guard turned away, Jagger was up and pumped two bullets into the back of his head.

Moving forward swiftly, he nailed the smoker, who had a deer-in-the-headlights look. Two bullets center mass. His body fell backward with a soft thump.

"You're all clear," Wendy said. "No one is looking out the windows or outside on either patio."

Still, he scanned the area as he hustled to the first trailer. Force of habit. He grabbed the handle and flung the door open.

Two guards were taking turns beating on a third man who was handcuffed to a chair.

Jagger aimed and shot, dropping them before they screamed for help. He swept inside, shutting the door behind him. "Who are you? Why does Vargas have you here?"

"I'm FBI. Max Webb. I was undercover in his organization. I'm part of the reason he was going to jail."

"Good enough for me." Jagger searched the pockets of the other men for the keys.

"Who are you?"

"Jagger Carr."

"Why are you here?"

Bingo. He found the keys and hurried to release the guy. "Emilio put out a blood debt kill order on my girlfriend." The word sounded so small and insignificant to describe what she was to him. "I'm here to resolve the issue." Although the FBI agent's presence complicated the matter. That resolution was looking more and more like it would come in the form of a bullet.

"Who's your girlfriend?" Agent Webb stood, rubbing his wrists.

"Wendy Haas."

The agent froze. "Haas? Any relation to Dutch Haas?"

"Yeah. You know him?"

"I do. Small world. I helped Dutch and Isabel Vargas once." Agent Webb pulled a Glock out of one of the dead guy's holsters. "You should get out of here."

"I can't. Besides, I think you could use the backup. I've got C-4 rigged to the middle trailer. Three guards inside. There's a fourth with a woman in the trailer farthest from the house. She looks to be innocent, maybe household staff. After I blow it, you take out the fourth guy and go call the cavalry."

"What are you going to do?"

"I've got unresolved business with Vargas." There were four more men inside the house standing between him and Emilio. Jagger was putting an end to the blood debt, come hell or high water. Nothing was going to stand in his way. He grasped the door handle. "Is it clear outside?" he asked Wendy.

"You're good."

"Ready?" Jagger asked the special agent, gun in his hand.

Webb gave a curt nod, holding the Glock.

They swept outside going in different directions. Jagger went around the side of the house to a patio door. It was unlocked.

"Headed inside," he said.

"Got it." Wendy's voice was a whisper. "Stay safe."

He took out the earpiece, shoved it into one of his cargo pockets and hit the button on the detonator.

WENDY JUMPED BACK as the middle trailer blew.

The explosion was startling, rocking the quiet. The fireball roared up into the dark sky. She'd nearly dropped the flare gun under her arm.

Swinging the binoculars back to where Jagger had been, she searched for him, but he was gone. Disappeared inside the house.

She pulled out the earpiece, and her body sagged with worry for Jagger. There was another man helping him now, but Jagger was still on his own in the house. By her count that left four more guards.

A chill slid down her spine, drawing her shoulder blades tight. It was the eerie feeling she had when someone was watching her.

She spun around and came face-to-face with Pilar and the barrel of her gun. Fear choked her as air backed up in her lungs.

Pilar came right for her. No hesitation. No banter. She seized the flare gun from under Wendy's arm and tossed it away. "Run and I shoot you. Scream and I shoot you." Pilar's cold eyes were narrowed in focus, her long dark hair was drawn into a slick ponytail, and she was dressed in black, blending in with the darkness. "Get in the truck, behind the wheel."

Wendy struggled to think, but the panicked rush of blood through her head made her brain cramp.

"Now!" Pilar said in a harsh whip of anger that got Wendy moving.

She got in the truck as Pilar climbed into the passenger's seat, keeping the gun pointed at Wendy's face.

"Drive to the house."

Wendy started the truck and threw it into Drive. Nerves took off in a wild dance in her stomach. "What are you doing here?"

"I got on the first flight this morning, at the crack of dawn. Last night, I baited Jagger. Dangled the lure of Emilio in El Paso. With your life on the line, I figured he couldn't resist. So, I came to reel in my catch and get the credit I'm due."

Wendy tried to control the anxiety welling inside her, but her whole body was shaking. "But why? You're friends. He trusted you."

"We are friends, but it doesn't serve my interests to remain friendly. I'm tired of my arrangement with Miguel, waiting for him to give me control of the Brethren. If I want the position, I have to take it. Show Emilio what I'm capable of. My value."

What a snake. "How did you know I was out here?"

"I've been lurking around the property all day. Spying on you while you scouted the place."

Oh, God. Her stomach clenched under a wave of nausea. "Emilio knows we're here? Jagger's walking into a trap?"

"No. If I had warned Emilio, then I would've had to ask permission to come. I'm more of a beg-forgiveness kind of woman. If Emilio had welcomed me with open arms, he would've let his men handle the situation, while pawing me, trying to turn me into his diversion in the desert." Her mouth twisted in revulsion. "No, thank you. That doesn't serve my interest either." Pilar's voice was pure steel. "But this little surprise does. These men... They look at me and see a mistress. It's time I opened their eyes to what I really am."

Panic slid through Wendy's veins. "What's that?"

"A cold-blooded mercenary."

JAGGER'S SIDE ACHED. He'd taken out three guards inside the house. One had hit him right in his wound, but he'd still managed to snap the man's neck.

There was one more guard. Jagger suspected the man was being a dutiful lieutenant and protecting his don.

Jagger was low on ammo. The submachine gun was empty. Only one 9 mm was fully loaded and the other was down to two bullets. At least he still had the smoke grenade.

He headed down the hall toward the office.

The door was closed. Most likely locked. He stopped in the doorway of a supply room short of the office.

After he squeezed off a couple of rounds, aiming at the lock, he ducked into the supply room just as the barrage of gunfire he expected came his way.

Hot slugs tore through the hallway. He got down on his belly, peered around the frame and smiled. All those bullets were eating up the door. It had already swung open partially and only chunks were left hanging from hinges.

Jagger popped the smoke grenade and rolled the canister down the hall. It clanked as it tumbled, landing in the office as the white phosphorous dispersed.

The hail of gunfire stopped.

Jagger hopped up and was on the move. He stormed down the hall, staying light on his feet so as not to make a sound, and charged into the office.

Through the smoke, he made out two figures shuffling into an adjoining room.

Determination fired through Jagger. He hustled forward, refusing to let them get away. Emilio Vargas was a disease, a cancer that brought misery and death.

It was time for this to end.

A lieutenant helped Emilio toward the patio doors in a small private living room. Jagger rushed them. The guard whirled around, jumping in front of Emilio.

Jagger pulled the trigger. The man stumbled backward, and Jagger squeezed the trigger again, punching another two rounds into the man's chest, sending him falling to the floor.

As Jagger shifted the muzzle to his true target, Emilio raised his own weapon, finger on the trigger, and pointed at Jagger's head.

They were locked in a standoff. If Jagger fired, Emilio would also be able to squeeze off a shot. Without a bulletproof vest, the gamble wasn't worth taking. Jagger needed to get him to lower the weapon first.

"This is over," Jagger said. "You're finished."

"I'm just getting started."

"The FBI agent is loose. He's in the wind, calling his buddies to come haul you back to jail."

"They'll have to find me first. I won't be sitting here waiting for them." Emilio edged toward the patio door.

"They will eventually find you. But I don't care about that. I care about Wendy Haas."

Emilio smiled, then his grin turned into a snarl, with teeth bared. "The blood debt must be paid. And you must answer for your betrayal."

"Or I give you the flash drive in my pocket. Records my father kept. Bank accounts. Documentation on your shell companies. Every detail of how you transport your drugs. It'll send Miguel to prison as well. For a very, very long time."

Emilio paled. "No. Not Warren, too." His gun wavered, but it didn't lower.

The muzzle was still pointed at Jagger's face. A shot would be fatal.

"Can no one be trusted?" Emilio said. "At least I'll no longer feel guilty about what happened to him in Venezuela."

Jagger's racing pulse slowed as the words sank in. "What really happened to him?"

Emilio's eyes hardened. "You'll never know."

The taunt was meant to throw Jagger off, have him spinning. His father was dead, and the truth wouldn't change it. He had to focus. No distractions.

"The flash drive is in my pocket. You agree to release Wendy from this debt and spare me, and I hand over all the evidence that would destroy the cartel. Miguel will stay safe." Jagger waited for an opening, for the gun to drop in the slightest. "Do we have a deal?"

Emilio's gaze flashed toward movement coming from the office.

Jagger pulled the second gun that was low on ammo and aimed at the newest threat.

Pilar emerged from the smoke. She had Wendy in front of her with a gun pressed to the back of her head.

Jagger's heart lurched.

"I have a better proposal," said Pilar. "Don Emilio gets the flash drive. I kill Wendy. He kills you. Then I take my rightful place as head of the Brethren." She yanked Wendy's head back, positioning her as a shield.

Even though Pilar's grip on Wendy's hair must've been painful, she didn't cower or cry.

"I'm sorry," Wendy said, her voice low but firm.

"Aww." Pilar's tone was mocking. "That's so adorable."

The situation was a powder keg. From this angle, Jagger's options were limited, but he had to get Wendy through this. He had to kill Emilio, even if it meant that Jagger wasn't walking away.

"What are you doing, Pilar?" Jagger asked, his gaze bouncing between her and Emilio, keeping a gun trained on each of them, knowing how vulnerable the position made him.

"Earning a promotion," Pilar said, full of ego. "No hard feelings. This is business." Her gaze swung across the room to Emilio. "What do you say to my proposal? You know how I love to be of service."

Jagger had been such a fool to trust her. She was using the discord between Emilio and Miguel, and exploiting Jagger's situation with the blood debt, to get what she wanted.

"Later, you'll tell me how you arrived in the nick of time. For now." Emilio smiled. "You have a deal."

One second everyone held their position, and the next, the room erupted into chaos.

A flash of movement on the patio caught Jagger's eye. Then a gunshot rang out. Don Emilio's body spun from the impact as he dropped the gun and staggered back.

Jagger glimpsed Agent Webb on the patio.

Pilar redirected her weapon outside, keeping a hand on the back of Wendy's neck, using her as a human shield while returning fire.

Jagger didn't have a clear shot. Damn it.

During the commotion, he caught Wendy moving her hand. She whipped out the switchblade from her pocket, pressed the button and jammed the knife behind her into Pilar's leg.

Pilar roared in pain as Wendy dove for the floor.

Before Jagger could seize the opening and pull the trigger, incoming gunfire from the window slammed into Pilar's chest, throwing her body backward.

Pilar hit the wall and slid down. Dead.

Wendy's eyes flared wide, filled with fear, but she wasn't looking at the dead woman. Jagger followed her gaze to the other side of the room.

Emilio had picked up his gun and was taking aim, with Wendy in his sights.

Jagger's heart clenched in his chest. In a blink, he raised his weapon and opened fire. At the same time, Agent Webb pulled the trigger, too.

Emilio took bullets from both men. Jagger didn't stop shooting until his weapon was empty. Emilio crumpled to the floor in a lifeless heap.

For a surreal second, Jagger was in shock. It was over. Don Emilio Vargas was dead.

"Wendy," Jagger called out, his eyes burning. He

reached her, dropping to his knees beside her, and pulled her into his arms. "Are you hurt?"

Wendy shook her head. "I'm fine." She cupped his cheek. "I was so scared."

"I'm sorry I let Pilar get to you." God, the thought of what could have happened to her made his blood run cold.

"I wasn't scared for myself. I was scared for you. That you might be walking into a trap."

Pilar had had a gun to her head and Wendy's concern had been for him. Not herself. She was an amazing woman with the biggest heart.

He kissed her. "That was quick thinking, using the knife."

"My brain shut down somewhere in the truck with Pilar. I just reacted."

"Still, you have impressive instincts."

"I can say the same about you, Carr," Agent Webb said, coming in from the broken patio door. "You took out a ton of men. Saved me a lot of pain, not to mention my life. I owe you. Big. What's your background?"

"US Army Rangers."

Webb nodded. "You did good." He knelt and checked Emilio's pulse, ensuring he was dead. "I called the police using one of the guard's phones. They've already mobilized and are on the way here with the local US Marshals." Webb went to Pilar and confirmed she was down permanently.

"But how?" Jagger asked.

"I don't know, a tip-off. Maybe good old karma." Webb looked around. "We should wait for them outside. Preserve the scene so we don't move anything by accident." He led the way out.

Jagger pushed to his feet and helped Wendy up from the floor.

"Thank you," she said.

"For what?"

"Everything." She wrapped her arms around waist and put her head to his chest.

With his arm around her shoulder, they made their way out to the front of the house.

"Jagger, now that I'm out of danger, do you plan to stick around?"

"I'm still a convicted felon. Being with me could complicate your life."

"Give the flash drive to Special Agent Morton. Better yet, we know a special agent that owes you big." She hiked her chin at Max Webb. "I'm sure he'd help you. After all, you did save his life."

Flashing police lights from a long line of cars were coming down the road.

"If for some reason, it doesn't work, and my record remains?" He leaned back, eyeing her, a frown tugging at his brow.

"Record or no record, we work. We've been through so much. Don't we deserve this, to be together, to have our second chance."

"Even if the cost is a major hit to your career?"

"I love you and I want to be with you. No matter the cost." She cupped his face and pulled him down for a kiss that made his knees grow weak, and his heart ache with joy.

They'd already paid such a high price. He wanted to start a future with her right now. "I do owe you a lifetime of kisses."

"And showers. Breakfasts in bed while we do the

crossword puzzle." She laid her head on his shoulder and he soaked in her warmth. "You once promised to get me a dog."

He had. Made lots of promises, and he wanted to make good on all of them.

The police and the marshals pulled up. Agent Webb spoke to them and directed one of the marshals over to them.

"Hello, I'm Deputy Marshal Laura Kirby, are you Wendy Haas and Jagger Carr?"

"Yes," they said in unison.

"Good. Your brother is going to be relieved to know that you're all right."

"Dutch?" Wendy straightened. "I haven't been able to get in contact with him."

"He was traveling, flying back from Alaska. When he landed, he was briefed on the situation with the cartel. He saw that you had called him, but he couldn't get a hold of you."

They had never turned her phone back on, not wanting to take the chance.

"But he had a missed call from a New York number he didn't recognize and called it back. He spoke with Tina Jennings. She gave him information that led us here."

Jagger looked to Wendy. "What did you do?"

"I wanted to help you and to see justice served if things went south."

He picked her up in a bear hug, kissed her cheek and then set her down. "Good instincts, honey. Don't ever doubt yourself."

"Let's get you two down to our marshal's office," Deputy Marshal Kirby said. "Your brother is expecting a phone call."

"I also need to speak to Special Agent Webb," Jagger said. Wendy's idea was great. He'd probably have better luck with Webb than Morton.

"You'll get a chance. They're going to bring him down to our office once he's finished here."

They followed Kirby to her car and climbed into the back.

He held Wendy's hand, and she put her head on his shoulder. The sense that everything was right in the world and the scales had been rebalanced came over him.

"Do you think the Brethren will leave me alone now?"

"Once they get word that Emilio is dead, yes, and after Miguel is arrested and his assets are frozen, they'll do what they can to help him avoid a conviction. But we should probably lay low for a bit, until the dust settles."

"Dutch will help us figure out the next step." She stroked his legged and he relaxed. "This whole thing has made me believe in fate. Like we're destined to be. As long as we're together, we'll be all right."

He tucked her in closer against his side. His heart was so full of love and something else he hadn't known in a long time—hope. "Well, we can't fight destiny."

Epilogue

Wendy walked through her town house in Arlington, Virginia, arm in arm with Isabel.

"It's gorgeous," Wendy said, holding up Isabel's hand, letting the sunlight streaming through the bay window reflect off her diamond engagement ring. "I'm surprised Dutch did such a fantastic job."

"I heard that!" Dutch called from upstairs.

"It was a compliment," Wendy said. "Not that you should be eavesdropping."

"I love how your wedding band matches your engagement ring," Isabel said. "It's gorgeous."

"Come up and take a look at it," Dutch said. "It's almost finished."

"Do you guys want some beers?" Isabel asked.

"It'd be kindly appreciated, sweetheart, after all our hard work," Dutch said, and Jagger grumbled loudly.

Wendy and Isabel both laughed.

"Go on up," Isabel said, "I'll grab the beers from the fridge."

"I could use the head start." Wendy stretched her back. She was so slow these days.

Taking her time, she ambled up the stairs and strolled down the hall. She turned into the room where the guys were. Dutch stood, leaning against a wall while Jagger was on his knees tinkering away.

She went to her brother and gave him hug. *Grateful* didn't even come close to expressing how she felt.

Dutch had paved the way with Special Agent Max Webb to have Jagger's record expunged in exchange for turning over evidence that not only put Miguel Vargas behind bars, but was also put the proverbial nail in the coffin for Los Chacales cartel.

As if that wasn't enough, he got Jagger a job at the US Marshals headquarters in Arlington, outfitting the government vehicles that they used for prisoner transport and fugitive apprehension. Jagger wasn't making the kind of money he had with Sixty, but it was an honest living and he was proud of his work, which would help keep marshals safe.

Wendy had relocated her PR firm to Virginia, and she had decided to do a complete one-eighty in how she approached things. No more social media. Her private life was private. Most of her clients were from Washington, DC, now, and by referral only. Less stress. Less hustle.

The change was good. Looking back, it was as though she'd been pretending to be someone she wasn't. Now she was more herself, the woman she was always meant to be.

Rising on her toes, she kissed Dutch's cheek.

Isabel came in with the beers and handed one to Dutch.

"Thanks, beautiful," he said, and Isabel beamed. They made such a great couple.

Isabel was beautiful and warm and kind, even though her father had been Emilio Vargas. Most important, she made Dutch happy, and her brother looked like he'd do anything for her.

Wendy sat in the rocking chair, watching Jagger tighten the last screw on his latest project.

"It's finished," Jagger said. "No thanks to you." He glared at Dutch. "I thought you came here to help."

"No, I came to visit my sister and supervise you."

Jagger stood up and tested his handiwork, shaking it to make sure it was sturdy. "Supervise? How many cribs have you put together?"

"None, but that's beside the point. I'm a natural-born leader, and I can see when things are going off the rails and corrections are needed."

Jagger rolled his eyes as Isabel laughed and handed him a beer. "Thank you."

Wendy rocked in the chair, looking around the nursery. They'd chosen a constellation theme. A starry night painting hung on one wall. Another was painted dark blue and had constellations drawn in glow-in-the-dark acrylic. She and Jagger both felt like the stars had aligned, or rather conspired, to give them a second chance and the baby boy growing inside her.

Orion, the hypoallergenic labradoodle they'd adopted from a shelter, crept in, even though he knew he wasn't allowed in the baby's room. He lay down beside her and curled up at her feet.

"You guys should consider getting a guard dog," Dutch said. "Like our Doberman, McQueen."

"McQueen is such a cool name." Jagger took a long pull on his beer. "But Steve McQueen was the king of cool."

"Amen," Dutch said.

Chuckling, Isabel shook her head. "He was named after Alexander McQueen."

"Who?" Jagger asked.

"The fashion designer," Wendy and Isabel said in unison.

Everyone laughed.

Wendy listened to the banter and laughter around her and had never been happier. This house, the dog, the crib, the life growing in her belly was all a manifestation of her deepest desires.

To have Dutch and Isabel to share it with them overwhelmed her with emotion. Tears filled her eyes and streamed down her cheeks.

"Honey, are you okay?" Jagger rushed to her and knelt in front of her. "Is it the crib? Do you not like it?"

"No, the crib is wonderful. You did a wonderful job." She whisked away her tears. "Ignore the pregnant lady. I cry at toilet paper commercials these days."

Jagger smiled at her, compassion and love gleaming in his eyes. Putting his hands on her round belly, he rubbed in circles. His touch was instantly soothing.

Later, he'd give her a foot rub and she'd sing his praises.

Before she started crying again, she looked up from Jagger and her basketball-shaped belly. "Are you guys coming for Christmas?"

"Definitely," Isabel said.

"Mom and Eric are also coming," Dutch said.

"And so is Tina." Jagger kissed her stomach. "It'll be a full house with baby."

"So, does your kid inherit ten million when he's born or when he turns eighteen?" Dutch asked.

Everyone chuckled.

"Either way, I'm going to be his favorite uncle," Dutch said.

"You'll be his only uncle." Wendy smiled at her

brother and silently repeated her current favorite word. *Gratitude.*

Hard to believe it had been almost a year and a half since the ordeal with Los Chacales cartel. The horror of it was a distant memory, but she wouldn't change a thing because her life was fuller and happier than she had ever dreamed possible.

* * * * *

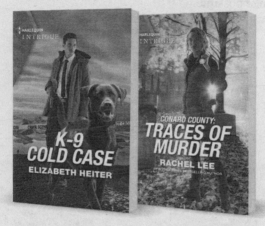

Desparre, Alaska, was so far off the grid, it wasn't even
listed on most maps. But after two years of running and
hiding, Sabrina Jones felt safe again.

She didn't know quite when it had happened, but
slowly the ever-present anxiety in her chest had eased.
The need to relentlessly scan her surroundings every
morning when she woke, every time she left the house,
had faded, too. She didn't remember exactly when the
nightmares had stopped, but it had been over a month
since she'd jerked upright in the middle of the night,
sweating and certain someone was about to kill her like
they'd killed Dylan.

Sabrina walked to the back of the tiny cabin she'd
rented six months ago, one more hiding place in a series
of endless, out-of-the-way spots. Except this one felt
different.

Opening the sliding-glass door, she stepped outside onto the raised deck and immediately shivered. Even in July, Desparre rarely reached above seventy degrees. In the mornings, it was closer to fifty. But it didn't matter. Not when she could stand here and listen to the birds chirping in the distance and breathe in the crisp, fresh air so different from the exhaust-filled city air she'd inhaled most of her life.

The thick woods behind her cabin seemed to stretch forever, and the isolation had given her the kind of peace none of the other small towns she'd found over the years could match. No one lived within a mile of her in any direction. The unpaved driveway leading up to the cabin was long, the cabin itself well hidden in the woods unless you knew it was there. It was several miles from downtown, and she heard cars passing by periodically, but she rarely saw them.

Here, finally, it felt like she was really alone, no possibility of anyone watching her from a distance, plotting and planning.

Don't miss
K-9 Hideout *by Elizabeth Heiter,*
available July 2021 wherever
Harlequin Intrigue books and ebooks are sold.

Harlequin.com

Get 4 FREE REWARDS!

We'll send you 2 FREE Books plus 2 FREE Mystery Gifts.

Harlequin Intrigue books are action-packed stories that will keep you on the edge of your seat. Solve the crime and deliver justice at all costs.

FREE
Value Over
$20

YES! Please send me 2 FREE Harlequin Intrigue novels and my 2 FREE gifts (gifts are worth about $10 retail). After receiving them, if I don't wish to receive any more books, I can return the shipping statement marked "cancel." If I don't cancel, I will receive 6 brand-new novels every month and be billed just $4.99 each for the regular-print edition or $5.99 each for the larger-print edition in the U.S., or $5.74 each for the regular-print edition or $6.49 each for the larger-print edition in Canada. That's a savings of at least 12% off the cover price! It's quite a bargain! Shipping and handling is just 50¢ per book in the U.S. and $1.25 per book in Canada.* I understand that accepting the 2 free books and gifts places me under no obligation to buy anything. I can always return a shipment and cancel at any time. The free books and gifts are mine to keep no matter what I decide.

Choose one: ☐ **Harlequin Intrigue Regular-Print** (182/382 HDN GNXC) ☐ **Harlequin Intrigue Larger-Print** (199/399 HDN GNXC)

Name (please print)

Address   Apt. #

City   State/Province   Zip/Postal Code

Email: Please check this box ☐ if you would like to receive newsletters and promotional emails from Harlequin Enterprises ULC and its affiliates. You can unsubscribe anytime.

Mail to the **Harlequin Reader Service:**
IN U.S.A.: P.O. Box 1341, Buffalo, NY 14240-8531
IN CANADA: P.O. Box 603, Fort Erie, Ontario L2A 5X3

Want to try 2 free books from another series! Call 1-800-873-8635 or visit www.ReaderService.com.

---

*Terms and prices subject to change without notice. Prices do not include sales taxes, which will be charged (if applicable) based on your state or country of residence. Canadian residents will be charged applicable taxes. Offer not valid in Quebec. This offer is limited to one order per household. Books received may not be as shown. Not valid for current subscribers to Harlequin Intrigue books. All orders subject to approval. Credit or debit balances in a customer's account(s) may be offset by any other outstanding balance owed by or to the customer. Please allow 4 to 6 weeks for delivery. Offer available while quantities last.

Your Privacy—Your information is being collected by Harlequin Enterprises ULC, operating as Harlequin Reader Service. For a complete summary of the information we collect, how we use this information and to whom it is disclosed, please visit our privacy notice located at corporate.harlequin.com/privacy-notice. From time to time we may also exchange your personal information with reputable third parties. If you wish to opt out of this sharing of your personal information, please visit readerservice.com/consumerschoice or call 1-800-873-8635. **Notice to California Residents**—Under California law, you have specific rights to control and access your data. For more information on these rights and how to exercise them, visit corporate.harlequin.com/california-privacy.

HI21R